LOST IN A VAMPIRE MOVIE

THE IMMORTAL ADVENTURES OF THOMAS JOHNSON: BOOK 1

OTHER BOOKS BY EILEEN RAYE

FOR ADULTS

Moonlight Walk on the Turtlestones

FOR CHILDREN

A Ghastly, Ghostly Night
Backyard Secrets Lost and Found

FOR YOUNG ADULTS

Alaine of Hawthorn
Lost in a Vampire Movie

LOST IN A VAMPIRE MOVIE

THE IMMORTAL ADVENTURES OF THOMAS JOHNSON: BOOK 1

EILEEN RAYE

Henderson, NV, USA

Dedication

To Steven Thomas, Jr., as Spock would say,

"Live long and prosper."

With Love,

Grandma

Acknowledgment

Greatest thanks to my editor Leanne Staback. In spite of an extremely busy schedule, she finds the time to help a friend reach a goal.

Without her keen eye, all of the sentences would be too long, and all of the commas would be in the wrong place.

Preface to a Horror Movie

*T*homas sat at one of the tables next to the railing of the cruise ship, which was gliding along on its way to Ensenada, Mexico. The ticket for the High School Graduation Cruise was a gift from his mother and grandmother, allowing him to join about three hundred others of his graduating class from Camarillo High School.

His stomach was full, and he sipped on his cola, listening to the dance music coming from the onboard nightclub. These cruise people sure knew how to feed their guests, he thought. He had a hamburger by the pool that afternoon, a dinner of several courses; and Josh, his roommate, had talked him into the midnight buffet. What a spread!

A breeze ruffled by and he could hear the engines churning in the black water below. A half-moon and thousands of stars were on display in the clear, night sky.

A solitary man approached the table, carrying a plate of food, and requested permission to share the table. Thomas nodded, taking another sip from his drink. Rather than starting to eat, the stranger started a conversation, gathering casual facts like where Thomas was from and how he was enjoying the cruise so far. Thomas answered, noting the man's accent, when Josh interrupted. He asked Thomas to join him at the nightclub - citing girls needed partners to dance. Thomas agreed to meet him shortly, saying he wanted to finish his drink and let his stomach settle for a few more minutes.

All the while, another man joined the man at the table and Thomas noticed that they were deep in conversation, speaking a language he didn't recognize. The first man apologized, introducing his roommate, explaining that they were Brazilian and on a holiday.

Thomas continued to sip his drink. He realized that he should probably go back to his cabin because he suddenly felt very tired. It was late and it had been a long day. He listened as the two men at the table now spoke in English, discussing their plans for the next day. Casually, they asked Thomas about his plans. Thomas couldn't think of the next day. A groggy feeling seemed to be spreading through his head and body. Finally, overwhelmed by a need for sleep, he laid his head in his arms on the table, thinking he would just rest for a minute before returning to his room.

Soon he was dreaming. Bad dreams consumed him. There were murmurs, black eyes, long, white teeth, pain and...burning. He tried to cry out, but his mouth was covered. The sharp pain was constant, coming from more than one place on his body at once. He tried to escape, but his body did nothing but flail about, unable to get free from the grip of the assailants. At last, he was freed from restraint. A burning pain remained, consuming him as if he were on fire, until unconsciousness claimed him. He sank into blackness.

Thomas awoke to the hum of a vacuum cleaner coming from the hallway outside the small cabin. He realized that he was naked, and almost any movement caused pain. He was lying on the cabin's only bed, tangled in sheets with blotched, red stains. The daylight was streaming in through the porthole and hurt his eyes. His mouth was dry, and his throat was sore. He remembered that he was on a ship, but this was not the cabin he shared with Josh.

The more aware he became, the greater the fear of what happened to him penetrated his being.

With effort, Thomas sat up on the side of the bed and tried to get his bearings. Feeling weak as he tried to stand, Thomas hobbled to the small bathroom and was shocked by his pale appearance in the mirror above the sink. His skin still burned as he began to examine the source of the discomfort. First, he saw the reddened areas on his wrists and arms that looked like inflamed insect bites, with welts on the top of the skin. His neck was bruised on both sides, showing patches of purple and blue. His naked torso, groin and legs also showed signs of assault. Waves of nausea and violent heaving hit him, and he leaned over the toilet. The vomiting went on and on, leaving his mouth and throat burning.

After several minutes, Thomas felt steady enough to get into the shower, where he found some relief as the cool water streamed over him. He let the water flow and turned his face under the stream.

Gradually, his consciousness was clearing, and an incredible terror was replacing confusion. An unbelievable myth offered its explanation for his plight. Vampires existed and he was an unwilling victim.

1

Black Hole in L. A.

The question was not if he was thirsty, the question was, how thirsty was he? The girl at the table next to him had been surveying him for the past thirty minutes as he read his text messages, worked on his journalism term paper, and did a few searches on his laptop. She was pretty with large, dark eyes. Possibly, she was wearing too much makeup. Her lips were nice - shaded rose - and she had a long, slender neck. She wore her clothes too tight, so no imagination was needed for what was under them. The young vampire summed her up as a typical, coffee bar groupie. She was the type of girl that was always trolling for the next hookup.

Thomas frequently came to Kafeene's Cup during the day. The coffeehouse lighting was minimal, so the surroundings were shaded, easy on the eyes, and gave a sense of intimacy. Small tables with computer jacks were secluded by large, leafy, green plants. It was usually a quiet place with New Wave music playing off somewhere in the distance. The coffee bar was close enough to the college to attract the local student clientele.

The girl's laptop was open in front of her, but Thomas noticed her eyes scanned the room frequently. She became aware of his attention and took the opening.

"Hi, you live around here?" she asked.

Nice voice, he noted. Thomas could smell the department store body wash from where she sat.

Hmmm…apple blossom, he guessed.

"Yeah, down the street," he responded.

Lame, he thought to himself. That would get you nowhere with the girl, but he was not passing out information today. He guarded his privacy and was careful not to give out personal details that could be remembered.

He knew that he had to be cautious when in his own back yard. This place was too close to home.

His mind wandered. Would he want to risk an afternoon quickie? Thomas knew he could easily convince the girl to take a drive down Kanan Road. Maybe they could make a stop along the scenic highway to look at the ocean views. Then, after a quick bite on her neck, he could leave her in a safe spot where she would wake up later feeling weak and wondering what happened.

Yes, he had developed his skills for mesmerizing people, especially girls, and was able to turn it on at will.

Snapping out of the daydream with the decision made, he logged off of his computer.

Get back to reality, man, he told himself. It was time to go home and make a beef liver smoothie to hold him until he could get some type O blood. He saw the girl's smile fade as he stood up and prepared to leave. He stowed the laptop in his duffle and headed to the door.

"See ya," he said, giving her a 'maybe later' look over his shoulder.

She might come here often, he thought, while putting on his sunglasses. The disappointment on the girl's face was obvious as she stared after him. He reached into his jeans pocket and pulled out a lemon drop candy, which he popped into his mouth hoping it would take the edge off his thirst.

Thomas preferred extra dark sunglasses to protect his sensitive eyes from the California sunlight. He usually wore a baseball cap, long-sleeved shirts and pants to protect his pale, thin, almost translucent skin. Contrary to the oversold myths surrounding his lifestyle, Thomas found that he *did* have the ability to move around freely during daytime hours, although it was uncomfortable for him at times. His mother's work allowed a routine for hours of quiet seclusion in his darkened bedroom, which she referred to as 'the cave'. Enhanced senses and agility naturally led him to feel better and become more active after sunset.

Thomas was still getting used to being a vampire, even though it had been almost two years since his change. Dealing with the constant need for blood was wearing on the soul — *if* he still had one. There was plenty of opportunity for a vampire with the large, local population.

Instead of leaving the area where he had grown up, and all that he had known, he decided to stay until 'the time was right to go'. He knew that he had plenty of time to take advantage of some of his new, shall we say, abilities. Jeez, he could make some money and buy a decent car, he thought, as he opened the door to his run-down Buick. The car's black, shaded windows provided extra protection from the afternoon sun, and he let out a sigh of relief as he moved into the driver's seat. He put the key into the ignition and slid the Muse CD into the dashboard, cranking up the volume for his favorite track.

Yeah, he knew about black holes - they suck you in. It was the story of his life. Staying home had its complications. There was family - he had an emotionally dependent, single mother with himself being her only child. He had a dog - a chocolate lab named Pismo.

He couldn't leave Pismo.

Rather than leave, he was biding his time. Thomas kept up the day-to-day charade by going to college and working part time at *Bluestone's* down in Malibu. All the while, he was dealing with finding blood on a regular basis. Summer break was coming up and he knew that he had to get some gig that would help with the cash flow. He needed a day job that did not require bright lights and sun.

What in the hell was a vampire doing living in southern California, anyway? People came here for the sun, but this had always been his home, and he was not ready to let go. He would continue to drag himself through the daylight hours, longing for dusk. He was a vampire hiding in plain sight, as they say.

Deep in thought, while merging onto the 101 Freeway going north toward Camarillo, he decided that he would keep the job at Bluestones even if it meant changing hours and taking less pay. He loved that job. He loved Malibu.

He was surrounded by the rich and famous nightly, and their perfectly styled daughters. Sometimes just the smell of them drove him crazy. His friend Brad had a father who worked there as a bartender and had put in the word for Brad and himself as parking valets. Parking anywhere near the beach was always a problem in Malibu, so they needed valets that could find safe parking places for the luxury Mercedes sedans, Beemers, and occasional Bentley or Ferrari.

His work hours were from late afternoon to closing time, which suited him. The valet lot was across Pacific Coast Highway - or PCH, as named by the locals - so there was a lot of trekking back and forth across the busy highway. He got juiced when he sped across in front of the oncoming headlights, daring them to hit him.

They'd screech the brakes, startled by the running image before them. They'd be left to wonder if they *did* see something, but he'd be gone. The tips were good at *Bluestone's*, and he was fast.

Last October, Mrs. Rielly - the owner of Bluestones - acknowledged that she had taken notice of him. One afternoon, before the early dinner crowd arrived, she called him into the small, messy, restaurant office for a chat. She leaned against the large, cluttered desk wearing a tight, orange dress, her breasts bulging at the low neckline. Her hair was bleached blonde and a little too long for her fifty-something age. Thomas had no doubt that the diamond jewelry she wore was authentic. She gazed up at him with a wistful smile, but then her eyes hardened for a more businesslike approach.

"One thing that I have learned over the years is that people in Malibu are either rich or they're rich and attractive. It costs money to live in Malibu. Not much low rent housing around here," she began, stating the obvious. "The natives appreciate attractive people. I've noticed that you always show up for work and can hustle when hustle is needed. You have a graceful way with the town's people."

She paused and watched him closely. Not knowing what she was getting at, Thomas decided to remain quiet.

"I'd like to offer you a job inside the restaurant."

The matron saw the surprise on his face.

"I've never waited tables," he said.

He felt that he needed to be honest with her.

"That's not what I had in mind," she said, smiling at him.

Was she trying to look sexy? Thomas wondered, as she stood up with one hand on her hip.

"I want you up front," she said, "Greeting the customers with your charming, X-rated smile."

The boss lady passed in front of Thomas, left the office, and walked down the short hall to the bar. He followed her closely. Going behind the counter to the register, she pulled out several bills and handed them to him.

"Go to Nordstrom's and buy two or three, nice, long-sleeved shirts and ties to wear with your black pants." She was looking at his face. "Blue would go well with your eyes," another pause, as if forgetting what she was saying, followed by awareness. "Can you come in at four o'clock tomorrow? Vickie will train you, so you'll be ready for Friday and Saturday."

Thomas looked down at the five, one-hundred-dollar bills in his hand and back up at her.

"Yes, I can do that," and he gave her one of those X-rated smiles.

So, Brad was left in the parking lot, while he became a host dressed in black slacks and tailored shirts, schlepping the privileged people to their tables. He learned to spot the tourists from the regulars. He made guests feel that they were getting a great-secluded spot, even for the worst table in the place. He instinctively knew who would be appropriate for the tables with a view of the beach.

Mrs. Rielly was happy with her choice and complimented him at the holiday party with a small, black box holding a diamond stud for his ear. She *did* keep an eye on him. Another available opportunity, Thomas thought. She was a very well preserved, middle-aged woman; but he wasn't *that* thirsty. No, he did not want to burn *that* bridge. He knew what he had to offer was not what she wanted.

* * *

Pulling the car into the driveway of the small house that he shared with his mother and the dog, Thomas remembered the text message she'd sent that morning, when he saw the plumber's van parked in front of the house. He opened the door and stepped into the living room. The carpet squished under his feet. The dishwasher had gone berserk and flooded the kitchen, dining area, and all the way to the front door of the small duplex they rented. He heard his mother talking to some guy in a blue shirt, with a picture of a big wrench on the back. She didn't sound happy. Evidently the guy had disconnected the dishwasher and pulled it out. He needed to get parts and would be back.

His mother didn't say hello, she just handed him a stack of towels to sop the water from the carpet. Thomas knew that life was going to be miserable for the next few hours. Since she was home, he wouldn't be able to make a bloody smoothie, so he popped another lemon drop into his mouth letting its sour tang placate his thirst.

"Go take a shower, Mom. I'll clean this up," he offered.

She gave him a hug and headed off to her end of the hallway. He got the sponge mop and systematically pushed the excess water out of the carpet and pad toward the kitchen, with agility and little effort.

Sometimes his immortal speed paid off as he quickly mopped the floor clean. He used the towels on the rug, sopping up any leftovers. He dragged the sopping throw rugs out to the back yard and hung them over the fence. The carpet was going to have to dry out, but he'd gotten the worst of it. After throwing all of the wet towels into the washer he slouched onto the couch and reached for the TV remote. He could hear his mother moving around at the back of the house.

Yep, he was twenty-one years old or would have been if his life hadn't been sucked out of him, and still living with his Mom. He knew that he would have to leave at some point, as he was forever stuck at nineteen and not aging, or he would have to tell her the truth. He wasn't sure how he could do that; so, for now, he stayed.

It had always been the two of them. His mother, Lynette Johnson, had never married his father. There had been some live-in relationships that hadn't lasted, but he still had hope for her to find someone for herself.

She was still young, just over forty. She didn't show her age, as she was thin as a rail with long brown hair, large brown eyes and only a few laugh lines. She had spent her life, so far, raising him and growing up herself. She had a young heart and mind. Sometimes, he felt like he had surpassed her and was the older one. He wasn't sure now who took care of whom.

The re-run of the Lakers game on cable wasn't holding his attention. Thomas knew that he needed to eat. Well, he still called it eating, even though his food source had changed. He knew every hospital within a hundred-mile radius.

Fortunately for him, health care was a priority in this town where hospitals were in good supply. He had added a couple surgical centers to his list recently, and now he was adding all of the larger dialysis facilities. They always had blood on hand. It's amazing what a lab coat and a clipboard could do for getting access to places during a busy time of day.

Thomas knew dinnertime was good for getting blood at hospitals. Everyone was busy, the personnel were changing shifts from day to night, and there were lots of visitors milling about. Most hospitals were laid out the same. His ability to move very quickly when needed was also helpful. Needing access badges was getting to be a problem, but he was starting to work on that. It was surprising how complacent people are with something that gets them through the doors. He already had a small collection of badges for various facilities.

Pismo sat next to Thomas on the couch. When he had first come home in his new state of existence, Pismo had shied away, sometimes whining. The large, chocolate lab had long since gotten used to him and would lie by his side to absorb the coolness from his skin.

Thomas's planning for getting some fresh blood was interrupted by his mother's voice.

"Do you want me to make you something to eat, Thomas?" she called from the kitchen, followed by, "Guess we'll have to use paper plates," she mumbled to herself

"No, Mom, I already ate," he replied.

She came to the doorway and gave him a tortured look. She was clueless, he thought. When was the last time she had seen him eat anything? He could see all of her thought processes regarding her supposedly anorexic son. She would be thinking back to Dr. Glenis, the psychologist specializing in eating disorders at the medical center. Glenis had lectured her about not pressuring her son to eat. Thomas could see that she was holding back.

"You should eat something, honey," she said, with her usual concern over his eating habits.

"I'm going with Kevin to watch the game. We'll get a pizza," he lied. "Don't worry, Mom."

She gave him a weak smile and went back into the kitchen.

He hated it when she beat herself up. His mother blamed herself for being the cause of his "anorexia". There were times when he felt he should just leave home and have a clean break, but that would probably be more painful for her right now, so he stayed.

Thinking back, Thomas tried not to come back home

after his vicious experience of being turned into a vampire. He managed to stay away and try to make it on his own for three weeks, only to end up a crumpled heap on the doorstep one summer morning. He was sick, hurting, and had nowhere to go. He was just starting to grasp some of the physical traits he had at his disposal for this new life form.

At first, he feared being around people for how he might react. Defeated, scared, and lying on the front porch, he was still wearing the same clothes that he wore when he stumbled off the cruise ship in Long Beach. An innocent, high school graduation cruise was where he met his life-shattering fate. Eyes burning and stomach in knots, he had been more terrified of his new world than it was of him.

He remembered seeing the shock on his mother's face when she first saw him, but she was beside herself with relief as she lugged him into the house. Her last three weeks had been any mother's nightmare. She had reported him as a missing person to the police and insisted that the Atlantis Cruise Line start an investigation.

The cruise to Mexico was a ship full of celebrating school kids. It was just a three-day cruise that was not supposed to end badly. Cruise line officials believed it was probably a tragic accident of falling overboard, which they proposed occurred from time to time. They assured her that they completed a full search of the ship when Thomas' roommate reported him missing on the second morning of the cruise. They reviewed all of the onboard camera footage to no avail.

The executives explained to her that no matter what precautions were taken on the ship, there was no way of stopping the consumption of liquor by the youngsters, and sometimes things got out of control. Not accepting excuses, his mother continued hounding them for a conclusive answer to her son's disappearance. She would never have given up on finding out what happened to her only child.

On that overcast July morning, his mother put Thomas to bed, while bombarding him with questions. She thought that he was in shock with his grayish pallor and cool skin. She wanted to take him to the emergency room, but he fought her on that, with true terror driving his argument.

At first, she checked on him almost hourly, peeking her head in the door. She called his grandmother, and they were debating whether or not they could get the family doctor to come to the house but had decided against it since he was so adamant that he would be all right. Resigned, she had allowed him to stay in his darkened room with the covers pulled over his head for two days. Attempts to feed him had failed, but he did seem to be drinking the milk and water that she left for him.

After two days of the self-imposed retreat, with thirst driving him nearly mad with hunger, he left the house after his mother fell asleep on the couch in front of the television. Pismo had growled in a protective manner as he passed behind the sofa.

Once out in the cool, ocean-flavored air, he ran into the hills above Camarillo. He knew the area since he had been there on hikes during his football training days. 'There's nothing like running uphill to build the leg and butt muscles,' his coach used to say; but Thomas was amazed at his new speed and strength.

He had seen a coyote, alertly watching him from behind a boulder. To his surprise, he was able to easily match and overtake the animal in seconds.

Instinctively, using his invigorated senses, his

descending teeth found the right spot on the neck, and he drank the blood as the poor animal died in his arms. He sat down on a boulder, stunned, looking at the creature that had been alive just a minute before while trying to face the truth about what he was… and would be from now on. He felt a sudden rush of warmth and exhilaration brought on by the warm blood; yet he mourned for the animal lying lifeless in his arms.

As the crescent moon shone down on the rural hillside covered with brush, Thomas realized that he could see every crack on a nearby rock, a lizard sitting statue-like twenty feet away, and a bird sitting in a bush, a hundred yards away. The vividness of the colors awed him, as he realized that he could see more acutely at night than during daylight.

For now, the greatest relief was the sated thirst. He felt revived, if that was possible; but in the back of his mind he knew that the thirst would return, again and again.

After a few weeks, he found that he felt better after he had satiated his thirst and was better able to cope with situations of trying to live with his new existence.

At times, in the beginning, he let the hunger get the best of him as he looked for victims to supply the blood he needed. He learned that he could not allow himself to get *too* hungry. He now knew how much blood he could take and still leave a person viable for easy recovery. Although his fear of discovery was a constant burden, Thomas soon realized that he had to find alternative sources for the human blood needed for his subsistence.

Enough dwelling on the past, he thought. Now, Thomas had his appetite and diet somewhat under control. He devised plans for a quick escape to calm the anxiety at being discovered as a vampire. He tried to put up a good front, like now, as he got up from the sofa, went into the kitchen and poured himself a large glass of milk. His mother was making some macaroni and cheese on the stove. He pulled the Hershey Syrup down off the shelf, gave a generous pour into the milk and began stirring with a spoon.

"You need to get some new pajamas, Mom," he teased. "The ragged look is out."

"What? You don't think the holes are sexy?" She was smiling as he walked out of the kitchen.

He walked down the hall to the bathroom, closed the door, and quickly dumped most of the milk into the toilet. His mother kept buying the groceries and he kept getting rid of them, while strategically leaving half-eaten articles of food around the house.

Pismo enjoyed it and had gained ten pounds, according to the last visit to the vet.

Thomas also continued his monthly sessions with Dr. Glenis, which seemed to please his mother. At this point, he was having fun toying with the psychologist. He gathered clinical information about the symptoms, and usual turmoil of anorexia, which is what he used as his cover story for not eating.

A minute later, he set the glass with the remaining chocolate milk on his bedside table and rummaged through his closet for a button-down shirt. He stuffed the white, lab coat into his backpack, which already held a clipboard and Los Arbores Hospital identification badge and went for the front door.

"Kevin and I are going to watch the game at *Leon's*," he called to his mother, who was now eating from her paper plate on the couch, while watching the news on TV.

"See you later," he said, going out the door.

Leon's was a local sports bar with a big screen and was always crowded on game nights. He knew that he would be off of his mother's radar for a few hours, as he headed for the car.

2

Leading Lady

Briana sat before the mirror in her dressing room at the television studio in Burbank. The small, crystal, Waterford clock on her dressing table said nine-thirty. It had been a long day for her, having gotten there at six- thirty that morning. One thing about acting in a TV show was that you stayed until the work was done, because the next day's work was already scheduled.

With relief, she took the elastic band out of her golden hair, letting it fall to her shoulders. She was tired and hungry. She could not face another piece of lettuce, even if it meant her stomach making lewd noises during the car ride home.

Thank goodness for the studio car and driver, she thought to herself. At least she didn't have to drive home at the end of the day. That was one studio perk that she was glad to have. She deserved it. She kept this TV show in the highest rating for four, long years.

It was a 'teenage' show, but the audience was probably a little younger. Pre-teens were an important demographic in America. *The Halls of Burton Academy* would live on in re-runs for years, depicting Briana's inescapable, juvenile image.

In the meantime, she was nineteen and done with it. The character she played, Cathy Bekins, was the student body president to a school full of academic misfits. The dialog on the sitcom seemed increasingly mindless to Briana, punctuated by stupid, adolescent stunts. She grimaced into the mirror.

She had been talked into another year with the show last year by Leonard Parker, the CEO of Rockface Studios. At the time, he promised crossover movies that would bring her into the young adult venue, but the scripts that she was offered were pitiful and more of the same juvenile, unsophisticated character types. They were either straight-to-video movie projects or more teen movies for airing on television.

Even her Aunt Joey, who was also her manager and agent, had to admit that none of the proposals were worthwhile in advancing her career. When the season wrapped up in two weeks she would be finished. If she never worked again, she knew that she had to remake her public image to be seen as a young adult. This was a sometimes-impossible transition for most child actors. The casting rooms of Hollywood were littered with kids that had been the stars of TV shows and movies. Originally selected for their clean looks and capricious personalities, they faded in desirability as they aged toward adulthood.

Briana came from a middle-class family of hardworking parents. She was the third child that had come along as an unexpected bonus for her parents - a little g i r l that was an animated, good-looking child. Her mother's friend opened the door for her to get into modeling as a toddler for department store advertising. Soon she had an agent. Her mother was forever dragging her here and there to business offices around Hollywood that looked at children for the entertainment industry. Since kids grow up so fast, there was an endless demand for new faces. It was a juvenile meat market.

Briana started working in television commercials at five years old. Then she was cast as a younger sister on a sitcom. She worked on that show for three seasons before it was cancelled. By fourteen she was a veteran and was offered her own show.

The Halls of Burton Academy was a hit for the studio. Her picture, with her school uniform and trademark ponytail, was soon everywhere from lunch boxes to school supplies, to her own line of dolls on the toy shelves. She feared that she would never be able to get away from her own manufactured, yet financially profitable image. Briana could end up a has-been before she was twenty. For now, her stomach growled, reminding her of its neglect.

Removing makeup, Briana sighed at herself in the mirror. She was nineteen going on thirty. Already she had been there and done that in the Hollywood world that ate people up and spit them out. She was well on her way to being a forgotten, teenage, TV actress, forever stuck in time – a character lost in re-run hell.

Teenager? What was that? She never really had the time to be a teenager. The years were lost to working. Now, she saw actresses younger than herself biting into the meaty roles she desired. Here she sat, tired and hungry, just wanting to get home and to bed before it started all over again tomorrow.

The door of the dressing room opened, and Briana's Aunt Joey entered carrying two bags from a nearby BBQ restaurant.

Briana looked at Joey and then the bags.

"Come on," Joey said. "We can eat in the car. Mario is waiting for us. We're late and he wants to get home before the *Midnight Show* comes on."

Briana did not have to be asked twice. The smell of the food spurred her on. With a last look around at her dressing room, she hastened out the door knowing it would all be here in the morning.

Located in the hills of Eagle Rock, a small community not far from the studio where she spent long hours, Briana had a house, bought and paid for with her earnings. She lived with her aunt since they convinced her parents to allow her to buy the house four years ago, mainly for proximity to the studio.

Joey Madison, who was her mother's older sister, the loving spinster was really the parent in Briana's life. Aunt Joey was the one person she could always trust to be there for her.

She got into the back seat of the limo with her aunt, tearing into the bag of food. Briana had not eaten since eleven o'clock that morning, and then it was a plain salad with a little vinegar dressing. She was supposed to be on a diet - the forever diet. She was not tall, a little over five feet, and maintaining her weight was an ongoing issue with too many people at Rockface.

A BBQ beef sandwich with curly fries was nowhere near her allowed food list. God, it was good!

Lights flew by the car windows as the limo sped east on the freeway. One good thing about leaving the studio late was that the normally congested freeway was free of traffic. Soon the headlights of the car reflected off the wooden gate at the front of the house while Mario entered the required code for the automatic opening. Decorative landscape lighting illuminated the front yard of the classic two-story home, with additional lighting along the walkway to the large, double, front doors.

Such was their routine, that once in the house, Joey went to her rooms on the first floor, and Briana climbed the stairs to her suite of rooms. Joey could hear the noise of a television emanating from Carla's room, their live-in housekeeper, as she got a glass of milk out of the refrigerator in the kitchen. Leaving the kitchen, she walked through the spacious, open-concept dining and living rooms toward her own bedroom and office at the other side of the house. Even though it was already late, she had to do some work in the comfortable office prior to going to bed.

Joey was responsible for all of the social media sites for Briana and wanted to do an end-of-day check for anything needing attention.

Fans thought that Briana communicated with them on the various sites. If they only knew, Joey thought to herself. Briana's contract with the studio was very restrictive and included controls on publicity and social media. Joey worked with the studio publicity department and used guidelines for any postings. In a few weeks, they would be out from under that contract, and there would be more freedom for postings.

Briana, unlike most teenagers, cared little for the various websites. She was nonchalant when told about the numbers of fans following her on the Internet.

Not that Briana didn't appreciate her fans, because she did, but she just preferred not to constantly put material out there regarding every thought and movement in her life.

Once home, Briana usually went to her bedroom. Actually, several of the rooms on the second floor had been modified for her use. She had a large, corner bedroom, allowing light to filter in the long windows on two sides of the room. The wall color was a soft blue, with creamy drapery flowing to the floor. Lavenders and pinks on the bedding and pillows added to the color palette. A puffy, grey sofa and chair with glass tables sat in front of a television, which provided a comfortable sitting area in one corner of the bedroom. Right now, her target was the large luxurious bathroom with a soaking tub and a glass-enclosed shower.

After a warm shower and slipping into a breezy, cotton nightgown, she stood in front of the bathroom mirror brushing out her blonde, shoulder-length hair one last time before going to bed.

Grabbing her script for the next day, she turned on the crystal bedside lamp and turned down the bed comforter. Once in bed, she did a quick read of tomorrow's lines.

What dribble, Briana thought to herself.

The show's writers, knowing that the show was ending, were just recycling ideas and dialog from previous shows, figuring no one would notice. Briana did care about the other actors and production crew that would be searching for work when the show ended, but she was counting the days for her release.

Turning out the lights, Briana let her mind wander to some of the things she wanted to do once the show was finished. There were so many things that were pushed aside due to her busy schedule. She wanted a break. She wanted time to go out with friends, go to a music concert, maybe even meet a guy and have a real date. Sugarplums danced in her head as she drifted off to sleep.

* * *

Thomas was not at the greeting podium in the Bluestones' entrance foyer when Briana Stillwood came through the restaurant's front doors. He was returning from seating a couple at an available table in the bar area. He stopped in his tracks when she appeared as recognition seeped into his brain. He took a sharp inhale of breath as a hush fell over the alcove filled with customers waiting to be seated for dinner.

Briana was not alone, but accompanied by a tall, thin, middle-aged brunette. Suddenly recognized, all available eyes were riveted to Briana, and necks stretched to capture a glance.

Thomas could not take his eyes off the young woman. Even in high heels she was probably less than five and a half feet in height. She was a vision in a simple, strapless, dark blue, taffeta dress that accentuated her slim waist, then flowed gracefully into a puffed short skirt that ended just above her knees.

Thomas's sight was sharpest in the dim light, and he engaged his ability of acute focus.

The girl's blonde locks were swept up in a sophisticated style. Her porcelain, oval face was looking toward the interior of the restaurant, with her sea-green eyes perfectly made up with just the right amount of shading and darkened lashes. Her small, straight nose was placed over well-shaped lips. She hadn't been afraid to wear a bold magenta lipstick. Sapphire and diamond earrings were her only jewelry, hiding part of her earlobe. Thomas's eyes were naturally led to the soft, creamy, column of her throat where a rapidly pulsing jugular vein belied the appearance of a calm demeanor.

This was not the girl Thomas remembered from Saturday morning TV shows. He stared at her bare arm, shoulder and upper back, as she was led away by Mrs. Rielly toward the restaurant seating area. His mouth was dry, and he had to concentrate to keep his bicuspid teeth from descending with unconscious anticipation.

Damn.

He popped a hard, sour, lemon drop into his mouth.

* * *

Briana and Joey were led to a table one step up on a riser

that allowed for an unobstructed view of the beach and waterfront. The sun had set, and the last pink shades of twilight were fading through the large, glass windows facing the shoreline. The table was narrow and seated six across the aisle from the row of tables lining the windows. The rest of the party was already seated. Briana took the center seat next to Margaret Siegel, Adam Siegel's wife, and Joey took the end seat. Pauline Mellick sat directly across from Briana, sipping her drink. Briana settled into her seat. Adam Siegel was sitting next to Pauline on the end, with elbows on the table, taking up more than his share of the table space. Putting down her glass, Pauline made the introductions.

Margaret Siegel, a middle-aged woman with dark hair and eyes, was perfectly groomed and dressed in a contemporary style, with multiple rings and bracelets alluding to her wealth and station.

Pauline, on the other hand, was dressed casually in slacks and a matching cashmere sweater set, with only a simple gold chain and gold, stud earrings. Her bob of auburn hair was styled attractively. Her nails were short, unpolished and she wore no rings. Few would perceive from her dress that she was one of the wealthiest women in Los Angeles, with an annual income that would put many millionaires to shame.

The table setting was cozy with small, potted candles illuminating the space under the dim, restaurant lighting. The pale blue tablecloth was adorned with shining silverware, and the faceted stems of the glassware sparkled in the candlelight. The lighting was kind to the three older women, but Briana's youthful beauty was startling and undeniable.

Margaret commented with approval on Briana's dress,

asking her where she had found it. The women commenced in small talk as Adam Siegel sat quietly sipping a drink, taking in the atmosphere and Briana.

Adam had just turned sixty-two and worked in the motion picture business since he was twenty. He came up through the ropes the hard way, working at whatever job he could get in the business, switching studios when opportunities presented themselves. He was savvy to the inner workings of his world. He and two other experienced producers had started Checkmate Studios eleven years ago, when Hollywood was going through a slump. Timing is everything in Hollywood. The right project, released at the right time, with the right actors on board, could fill movie theater seats and make lots of money.

The new studio had been lucky. Several early projects had paid off which gave them the necessary recognition and credibility. Checkmate had the ability to attract good scripts and talent. Currently, they had several 'A-List' stars signed on for projects. Most of all, with a good track record, Checkmate was able to get funding for the projects.

Deals were also on the table with several well-heeled stars that wanted to produce their own projects but needed backing. Checkmate Studios helped with the marketing and distribution for them, taking a cut on the box office. Making movies was always a gamble, as the audience was very fickle, and often the movie made just enough to pay for its making, and sometimes less. Now that film projects were so expensive, less films were being made by the big studios every year.

At the front of Bluestones, Mrs. Rielly smiled to herself having caught Thomas's reaction to the young actress when she entered the restaurant. She was a little surprised since she had observed his behavior over the past year and never saw him lose his composure over a girl. Just the opposite was true. All of the female staff, even the older, married waitresses had taken a shot at him, only to be politely rejected.

He was friendly, but aloof. He did not participate in the workplace gossip that went on whenever you get a staff of young people together. Rumors had gone around that Thomas did not like girls, but Mrs. Rielly's sixth sense told her he was heterosexual. For some reason, he kept to himself, rarely giving any clues or insight as to what was really going on with him. He didn't speak of his life outside the restaurant, and he had never, to her knowledge, had any outside contact with other staff members.

When she returned from seating the starlet, which was causing a wave of hushed whispers throughout the foyer, she went to her reserve wine closet and pulled a bottle of 1980 Napa Valley and waited for Thomas to return to his post. It was not long before he came to stand beside her at the desk.

"So, do you think she's hot?" his boss whispered to him.

Thomas looked down at his shoes.

"That was an opened mouth stare on your face if I ever saw one," she teased.

"Well, she does look really different than she does on that stupid television show," he said, as if trying to explain himself. "She's so grown up."

"And good looking," the restaurant owner added.

"Ah, yeah."

"Want a closer look?"

She looked up at him with a little smile and crinkles at the corners of her eyes.

Thomas looked at her but was not sure what she was expecting as a response.

"Here," she said, handing him the bottle of wine. "Take this to the table, compliments of Bluestones. Be sure to open it for approval by Adam Siegel."

Thomas had done this many times before. Mrs. Rielly frequently thanked important clients for their patronage and kept a closet of wine for those occasions. Thomas hesitated, trying to not appear too eager.

"I have a couple of tables opening up. I'll seat them and then take the wine."

Mrs. Rielly smiled. She really liked her favorite host.

At the table, Adam Siegel was there to support Pauline, whom he jokingly referred to as his 'other wife'. Pauline wanted to break into some less serious projects, marketing to the teen and young adult audiences. The young adult market had exploded in the past few years, with some of these films being some of the top money makers. Adam trusted Pauline's instincts, which had brought him a lot of success over the years. His feelings for her ran deep and they were close, but their relationship had always been above reproach.

Adam separated his family and work life. At home, his wife ran the show, taking care of him and the family, which allowed him to focus on work. Margaret and Pauline were the women in his life, and they got along well, which was rather amazing for the Hollywood crowd. Adam was a Jew and held to his faith, where Pauline was an Irish-Catholic originally from Boston. She had never remarried after one treacherous marriage in her youth. She never had children, but she was an established 'Aunt Lina' to Adam's brood of four, never missing birthdays, holidays, or Bar Mitzvahs.

Pauline was taking the lead on this project, and Adam wanted it to work for her.

During a lull in the ladies' conversation Adam directed his attention to Briana.

"So, I hear that the contract on your TV show is up and that you're looking for more adult acting roles?" The table chatter ceased, and all became quiet and attentive.

"Yes," Briana responded. "Rockface Studios has offered me a couple of projects, but they were more of the same juvenile types of things that I've been doing."

She paused.

"And I'm so identified as the Cathy Bekins character with her ponytail hair and the *Halls of Burton Academy*, I'm not sure if there is a chance of doing other things after that show. I'm looking for parts that are a little more adult."

Briana looked Adam straight in the face. She would not let him think that he could intimidate her. She let the Rockface Studio head intimidate her last year and ended up with another year on a TV show that she had not wanted to do.

"I wouldn't mind a small character role that would allow me to do something different," she added.

The girl's humility served her well. Everyone at the table knew that Rockface had made a bundle on the show and all of the merchandizing associated with *Burton Halls*. Briana was not new to the business and had proven herself by dependably delivering for Rockface over the past five years.

"Do you think that you could carry the lead role in a movie?" Adam asked.

"Yes, I think I'm ready for that," she answered with a

decisive tone.

Pauline joined in. "We have a project that we're gearing up on for release next spring. We're trying for the Memorial Day crowd. It's scheduled to start shooting in June. We have the director signed and are working on casting. The script is done, for the first draft. We're getting ready to look at locations, and story boarding is pretty much finished."

No one spoke, so Pauline continued.

"This project is a romantic thriller geared for the high school and young adult crowd. We want to keep it pretty clean to avoid any restrictive rating that would decrease the size of the target age group, so there's a roller coaster of action and thrills with some romance."

"Sounds exciting," Joey commented, in a noncommittal manner.

"The story is about a young, disoriented man with no memory, found on the side of the road by our heroine. Not long after trying to nurse him back to health, she finds that he is strange in many ways. In the meantime, he starts to remember things and is having flashbacks that make him realize he is a vampire, and that evil fiends are after him. Of course, they both have a strong attraction for each other that leads to romance. Enter bad guys and the hero becomes aware of his supernatural abilities. Of course, the evildoers are now after our heroine as well, who is saved by her young, dark hero. The bad guys are eventually destroyed, just in the nick of time." Pauline paused.

"That's pretty much it, in a nutshell," she said, waiting for a response.

"Hasn't that been done before?" Briana asked.

"Well, yeah, it's been done before, and *it works*," said Pauline. "The script is the key. It was written by Carry Sloan, who seems to be able to get the right balance for the romantic thriller that both adolescent boys and girls would appreciate. Do you think that you might be interested?" Pauline asked, looking at Briana.

"Yes," said Brianna. "I'm definitely interested and would like to read for the part, if possible."

Just then a handsome young man came to the table holding a large bottle of wine, which he showed to Adam.

"Compliments of Bluestones' management," he said in a warm, clear voice.

All at the table paused to watch as he adroitly opened the bottle and poured a small amount of the dark, red liquid into Adam's wine glass. Adam approved the wine, and the young host poured Margaret's glass halfway from the top, then Adam's, and proceeded around the table until he came to Briana. Their eyes met as he deftly lifted her glass and poured the remainder of the wine, then held the glass out for her. Everyone at the table - and on the planet - knew that this famous, young woman was not of legal age to have wine.

She smiled sweetly as she reached out to take the glass, never breaking her gaze from the server's face. Her fingers brushed his, which were cool, and she noted the sensation in her being. It was only a few seconds of time, but the two were lost in the moment and in each other.

"Thank you," she said, in almost a whisper.

Thomas broke free of her gaze, lowering his eyes and turning away from the table. He walked back up the path between the tables with a stunned look on his face and an empty bottle in his hand.

Briana, feeling flushed, was lost in her world. After a few seconds, she sighed and took a sip of the illegal wine.

Adam coughed.

Margaret adjusted herself in her seat.

Joey, closest to Briana and most in tune as to what had just happened, resumed the conversation with Pauline as a distraction by asking, "So, do you think that we could have a look at the script for the movie?"

"Sure, I'll send it to you Monday, as soon as I can get an extra copy," said Pauline, but her mind was elsewhere.

She had not missed the electric exchange between the young beauty and the man with the piercing, dark eyes. The expressions on their faces were raw, lost, seeking, tender and unexpected. That was the exact chemistry she needed for her project.

3
Paparazzi

Carlin DeRossi couldn't help but notice the large, white orb ascending in the evening sky over the Malibu coast as he walked along the side of Pacific Coast Highway. It was a little jaunt from the half mile away from where he was able to park his car. The double, front doors of the Bluestones Restaurant were in sight now, and he shifted the camera strap hanging around his neck to make sure that all was hidden under his coat.

The spring evening was cool with a slight sea breeze. The usual cloud cover that closed in on the coast this time of year had stayed out to sea. The lure of the full moon tugged at him and made him want to be elsewhere pursuing his own pleasures, but tonight that was not to be. This was work, with a promising paycheck. *Get the picture* - that was his job and why he had an appointment at the restaurant. He was one of the best at getting the right picture, of the right person, and *that* gave him the right price.

DeRossi hadn't planned to work tonight, but as it sometimes happened in his line of work, a tip had come out of the blue. Actually, a voicemail was left on his machine on his condo's landline. *It was worth every penny to keep that phone*, he thought to himself. The message had been brief. An unidentified female voice left the cryptic message, 'Briana Stillwood will be at Bluestones Restaurant in Malibu this evening with a notable dinner companion.'

This was what he lived for - exposing the real people behind the trumped up, larger-than-life personas made up by the Hollywood machine. Briana Stillwood was just at the age when the veil of innocence was ready to be lifted. So far, her image was squeaky clean. Maybe tonight would show another side. Even though she was a popular child star, candid shots of this girl were rare. She was usually only seen at very controlled, media events. Rockface

Studios made sure that their interests were protected. The studio was even more vigilant now that Briana had blossomed into a striking young woman, holding on as long as possible to the famous, girlish image. The gossip tabloids and Internet were full of these debutantes being caught with their pants down, and he was just the person to provide the fodder for the fire.

DeRossi opened the restaurant door and walked into the foyer filled with people waiting to be seated. He avoided the front desk and turned left into the bar, which was also crowded. That was all the better for his intentions, providing cover to observe and not be seen. The hum of low voices filled the air. He found a lone bar stool that - with a small swivel - allowed him to survey the busy restaurant scene. He was not sure *what* he was looking for, but he did know *who*. He methodically focused his attention, going from table to table, until he found his mark.

Actually, the face that first registered was not Briana Stillwood, but Adam Siegal - one of the founders of Checkmate Studios - and next to him, Pauline Mellick. Yes, he recognized Siegel and his cohort Pauline. DeRossi's business was to know the names and faces that made up the entertainment industry. Siegal and Mellick were rarely seen together in public, so the photographer could readily assume that this was a business dinner.

A dark-haired woman sat across from Siegal, and the photographer realized that the back of a blonde-headed person in the middle seat had to be the young Miss Stillwood. Another woman sat on the other side of her, possibly her agent.

Yes, this was a business meeting, he confirmed to himself. Many deals in the industry were made over a lunch or dinner with a few cocktails thrown in for good measure.

It looked like there would be no scandalous revelations about Stillwood tonight, so the price for any photo would be far less than he had allowed himself to hope. However, this may still be news regarding the young star. There could still be a market for a candid shot of the girl, so he would wait. He planned to be ready when she got up to leave, and he would get the picture as she was on her way out of the restaurant.

* * *

Thomas went into the kitchen to dispose of the empty wine bottle after leaving the table with Briana Stillwood. He was emotionally shaken for being so drawn to the actress. His reaction to her scared him, but he pressed it down and composed himself. Briana had looked at him as if she knew him, and they were close.

No, it was just his imagination, he thought. Now he understood the phrase 'star-struck'.

Shake it off, man, he told himself. *Remember what you are. That girl could never be used for a quick source of blood. Vampires don't have friends, or girlfriends.*

Returning to his post, Thomas noticed a solitary man come through the restaurant's entrance. A strange sense of alert hit him, and he zoomed in. The man didn't approach the desk to put his name in for a table but turned directly toward the bar. Maybe the guy was meeting someone, Thomas thought to himself.

The man was under Thomas' six feet in height. He was wearing a black coat, like a trench coat, or maybe a raincoat.

What's that about, Thomas wondered, as it was a clear night and not overly cool. Trench coats were certainly not a current style. It gave the stranger a sinister air. Beneath the coat, he wore a black shirt with dark pants. Thomas's sharp eyes followed the man as he made his way through the bar and seated himself on a barstool, only to turn partially away from the bar to gaze into the restaurant.

His hair was dark and receded sharply on both sides of his forehead leaving a dark clump of hair in the middle. His forehead had one deep line traversing the space above the dark eyebrows. The shadowed eyes were dark and searching.

Who was he looking for, Thomas wondered, and was he up to something?

The man's skin was tan and closely shaven except for elongated sideburns in front of his ears. The sideburn brought attention to a small, red, teardrop earring hanging from his left earlobe. His mouth was thin and set as his eyes searched the restaurant diners. Whoever this guy was, Thomas was sure that he was not a local…*or a* tourist.

He was pursuing someone, Thomas guessed. Maybe he was a private detective, which would not be unheard of in Malibu, where marriages didn't always end well when large amounts of money were involved.

Thomas kept an eye on the man with the teardrop earring, in between showing patrons to available tables. The guy hadn't moved - he just sat on the barstool, glanced at the basketball game playing on the TV over the bar, while holding a beer. Thomas saw him making side glances into the restaurant area every now and then.

Suddenly, the man stood up, plunked down some money on the bar and made his way toward the entrance foyer.

At the same time, Briana was coming up the aisle closely followed by Adam Siegal. Thomas was watching

Briana, and didn't notice the short man position himself directly in front of Briana and Adam. A camera appeared from beneath the coat and all of the questions were answered when the flash went off several times in quick succession.

Thomas went into action, immediately stepping between Briana and the man with the camera. The man stepped forward in a challenge to go around him. Thomas raised his arm, and the man ran into what seemed like a steel bar. As they clashed, Thomas looked down into the man's dark eyes and a sense of fear hit him and he recoiled backwards. The man's determined stare focused on Thomas, and a look of surprise dawned on his face. He also moved backwards. Staring at one another, neither man anticipated physical contact.

As if on cue, Adam Siegal stepped forward and took command of the situation. Siegal was a big man and was used to having the occasional spotlight.

"What paper do you usually work for?" directing his question to the man with the camera.

The photographer straightened and turned toward Siegal.

"I freelance," he said, in a surprisingly deep voice.

"Well, Miss Stillwood and I wouldn't mind having a photo or two taken, would we?" Siegal said, turning to Briana.

Briana smiled and understood the studio mogul's meaning. A picture with Siegal would be just the thing to shake up the 'suits' at Rockface. She stepped closer to the famous producer, who put a fatherly arm around her shoulders, and the photographer took a few good shots. Then Adam Siegal went on to let the small crowd of onlookers know that he was hoping to be working with Miss Stillwood in the near future. He added that a Checkmate Studios project was being developed especially for the star, which would allow her to stretch her wings in a movie role. He went on to shake the photographer's hand and ask him to try to get a good magazine for the photos. The photographer disappeared out the door with the Siegal party not far behind.

Thomas was shaken but went back to his post.

What a weird night, he thought to himself. Images of Briana kept surfacing, between memories of a strange, little man with an earring.

Maybe he needed blood, he thought. No, he felt like he needed to run. Energy had built up inside him that needed to be released. He glanced at the nautical clock on the wall over the entrance alcove, silently counting the hours until closing time.

* * *

The rays of moonlight streamed in through the two, elongated windows providing a silvery coating to everything in Briana's large, second-floor bedroom. Briana was on her side in bed, with a pillow pulled to her chest as she gazed toward the shafts of light. She couldn't go to sleep. The events of the evening were racing through her mind. She was trying to commit every moment to memory. As she thought about the interactions with Adam Siegal and Pauline Mellick, she could not help but be excited at her first chance for a lead role in a film. This was just what she had been hoping for.

Her Aunt Joey had been less excited during the car ride home from the beach.

"We're going to have to wait and see the script and look at the offer on paper before we commit to anything," Joey had said. "Let's see what they're willing to give you."

Although it looked good initially, the whole momentum of her first film project needed to be right, or she could be washed-up after one film. Many famous child stars became very forgettable after their attempts at an adult career. Briana knew that her aunt was right. She had been in the business long enough to know that everything boiled down to the written contract. Sometimes it was not what *was* said in the contract, but the things that were *left out* that could cause headaches. Joey always ran the contracts through their attorney prior to signing.

Briana wondered if the pictures taken at the restaurant would make it into the Internet blogs or any of the high-profile magazines.

That had been a surprise, she thought. *What a strange man*, she wondered as she remembered the photographer.

She searched her memory, but never remembered seeing him before at any of the press events. Tonight's initial attack for photos had been like an ambush. The photographer must have somehow known that she would be there and had been waiting for her. Even though she was very well known as a TV celebrity, she couldn't remember the last time that a photographer tried to take her picture outside of a publicity event.

Finally, Briana's thoughts went to what she had tried *not* to think about all night - *that guy*.

Who was he? Why couldn't she meet someone like him? When he poured the wine, he obviously didn't look at her as a child. She tried to remember the details of his face. His eyes were so captivating they seemed to hold hers. When she had accidentally touched his hand, a bolt of energy went through her.

At that moment, she wanted to forget the importance of the business meeting and all of those around her. She just wanted to talk to him. Then again, when they were leaving, he had jumped in front of the photographer, trying to protect her. With all of that, she never had a chance to speak to him.

Her thoughts strayed. She imagined walking along the beach in the moonlight, holding hands with the captivating, young man; or, to have someone like him put his arms around her.

How do you ever get to know someone like that, she wondered? She was so isolated in a trap made by the studio and her fame.

Guys did sometimes hit on her; but they didn't really know her, and Briana was frequently cautious regarding their real motives. So often these were young actors just starting out in the business. She was not sure if they really liked her or just wanted to be seen with her for their own ambitions.

Maybe she could go back to the restaurant to see him again. What if she did? She wondered. What would she say to him? She sighed and hugged her pillow. She would have to be satisfied with reliving the evening's moments in her mind. She would try to remember every detail about the intriguing stranger with the deep blue eyes and tuck it away for her dreams.

* * *

Thomas rushed out of the restaurant at his first opportunity near closing time, not hanging around to do any last-minute tasks. With a fast pace, he got to his car and made a getaway, speeding north on the Pacific Coast Highway rather than taking his usual route home up Kanan Road.

After a minute, he slowed down, remembering that this stretch of road was highly patrolled at night, and he didn't want to see any red lights in his rear-view mirror. Cops watched for the fancy, need-for-speed sports cars that haunted PCH – not that they would be interested in *his* aged mode of transit.

He drove toward Ventura, where Thomas knew of a stretch of beach that provided a long expanse for a run. He felt like a spring that needed to be sprung. The moon was high in the sky and moonlight flowed onto the highway. He glanced out at the ocean and saw the reflection of the light on the dark water.

After about thirty minutes, he did a U-turn on the highway and pulled to a stop along the side of the road. Thomas got out the car and climbed down the steep bank onto the beach. His senses were alive as he breathed the sea air deeply, enjoying the scent of the ocean. The waves were mild, performing their rhythmic run onto the shore. Thomas removed his shoes and socks and turned up his pant legs. He had already left his dress shirt and tie in the car.

Thomas ran down to where the water and the sand merged and began his run. He started with a burst of speed, pushing himself to cover as much sand in as little time as possible. After a few minutes, he slowed his pace, taking in his surroundings.

At one point, he ran by what looked like a smooth, large mound of rocks sticking up right at the water's edge. He wasn't sure what it was, so he circled around for a closer look.

No, it was not a smooth rock, it was an animal. Thomas remembered that sea lions frequently were seen along these beaches, but as he drew nearer, he saw that it was not a seal. It was a dolphin, beached on its stomach, seaweed surrounding it on the sand. It was at least six feet long, and the waves coming in halfway up the body from the tail. Its eyes were open, and the beak-shaped mouth was also slightly open so that the shadow of sharp little teeth could be seen.

At first, Thomas thought that the animal was dead, but when he touched it near its blow hole, the dolphin moved and took a breath.

By reflex, Thomas jumped back. The animal was alive.

Thomas sat down on the sand about six feet away from the mammal. He watched the dolphin take the occasional breath of air and stir from one position to another. Empathy overtook Thomas as he watched the animal struggle. The dolphin was alone, stuck in a place it didn't belong. It wouldn't last long once the tide went out and the sunshine beat down on its back.

He understood how it was to be in a world where you didn't belong. He knew what it was to be alone…always alone.

Thomas jumped up, undid his belt and removed his pants, leaving only his briefs. He walked up to the animal while trying to judge how to get it back into the water. First, he grabbed the tail, which was immediately thrashed out of his hands as soon as the dolphin felt under attack. Thomas tried again, this time getting a grip right above the tail and pulled the animal into the shallow water. The dolphin started to move around, as if trying to swim, but the water was too shallow. Now in the water, the mammal appeared stronger.

Thomas positioned himself alongside the body, behind the head. He didn't want to get bitten. In one swift movement, he bent down and gripped his arm around the body of the dolphin. With effort, he moved toward deeper water. Once in the waves, he tightened his grip and dove into the water, swimming with his legs and free arm. The animal was struggling against him, but his hold was sure as he made his way out into the open water lugging the beast.

The ocean was inky, but Thomas was close enough to the surface to see the moonlight penetrating the darkness. Continuing to struggle, the dolphin wanted to be free from his grip. Thomas kept swimming, hoping that he could get far enough out that the animal wouldn't once again go toward the shore.

Suddenly, another dark shape appeared alongside him that caused Thomas to loosen his grip. The dolphin took advantage of the moment and quickly slipped away from his reach. Fear hit Thomas as he realized that the dolphin was free and could come after him, and that another dolphin had joined them, swimming near the rescued animal.

Thomas swam toward the surface of the water and broke through to open air. The animals followed and Thomas saw two other fins appear nearby. He was surrounded.

Had they been waiting for their companion? He wondered.

A dolphin head surfaced within a few feet, then another. The mammals had their chance to go after him, bump him, or try to take him down, but they didn't. Thomas turned his body toward the beach and began to swim. The dolphins stayed by his side for a time, but finally broke off and disappeared into the night.

Later, sitting back on the beach, drying off in the sea breeze, Thomas reflected on the experience. He wondered if he'd saved the animal. He wanted to think so. The dolphin was off to swim in the moonlight and Thomas felt he had made a difference.

The night was long, and Thomas was starting to feel tired. The sun would be coming up in a few hours, and he needed to think about getting some blood. Absentmindedly, he wondered if there was anyone to save him.

* * *

DeRossi looked into the bathroom mirror rubbing his jaw. It was just a little after nine o'clock in the morning and it had been a successful night. He busily moved about his modern condo through the early hours, processing the recently taken shots of the prior evening in his darkroom. The pictures of Briana Stillwood were successfully sold to three websites and two teen magazines. One industry insider paper promised a mention on their evening entertainment news show using the photo. A busy morning, it helped to be able to provide Adam Siegal's comments about a possible working relationship between Stillwood and Checkmate Studios.

DeRossi left the bathroom and moved toward the bed, drawing the window shades against the morning sun. Much to his satisfaction, it had turned out to be a profitable night. He would get up later that afternoon and head out to one of the many hot spots he haunted, following the current Hollywood buzz.

* * *

Carol Berman sat at her wide desk going through head

shots when one of her three phones rang. It was the land line in the A. M. Casting office. She and her long-time business partner, Ann, shared the large executive-style office within the business suite. On a Saturday morning, she would usually let the machine take the message, but she automatically reached for the receiver and picked it up.

"A. M. Casting," she answered, continuing to go through the pile of actor's eight-by-ten, colored photos she had pulled for a current job.

"Carol, this is Pauline," the voice waited for recognition.

"Hi, Pauline," Carol answered, abruptly coming to attention.

From her experience, a call from a producer on a Saturday morning was probably not a good thing.

"How are we doing with the vampire movie?" Pauline Mellick got right to the point.

The vampire movie was currently under the working title *Lost Vampire,* poised to be a romantic thriller and possibly the breakout movie for Briana Stillwood. The target audience was teenagers and young adults. The movie currently had a budget of seventy-five million, which was pretty low by current standards, especially when computer generated, special effects were involved.

If Briana signed on, she would be the box office draw and would be taking home a hefty paycheck. Part of A. M. Casting's job was to assemble a cast of actors that would support Briana and sell to the young crowd. Carol's agency was focusing on young actors with some experience, but who hadn't yet achieved a 'known' status outside the industry. Salaries for these people could be negotiated at a union scale rate. Hollywood was a union town.

"Well, we have some really good candidates for the supporting roles ready to look at, but we are still working on the male lead. We have a couple young actors with some good experience that we've taped for the role opposite Briana."

Carol knew that the director for the movie was already in pre-production, and would have a strong say related to the final casting

"Actually, that's why I'm calling," Pauline continued. "Adam and I have a male lead prospect that we would like you to work up. We think that he would show well with Briana."

Carol knew Adam Siegal was the *name* producer behind the project. People were willing to put money down based on his track record with lucrative box office hits. Pauline was the quiet, behind-the-scenes producer that worked closely with Siegal and had been putting up at least half the money on his projects for the past thirty years. Everyone in the business knew Pauline and her influence, but few outside the industry knew who she was, other than a name appearing frequently on the credits of the films.

Carol wished she had not answered the phone because this was the dreaded call that all casting directors hated to get.

"Please don't tell me he's…" Carol started to say.

"Yeah," Pauline interrupted. "He's as green as they come."

"He's not an actor?" she questioned, sinking into despair. "Is he related to someone?"

These types of things usually led to expensive and time-wasting workups, only to be rejected for a more experienced, possibly unknown, actor. Not to mention she already had Siegal's niece - a supposed starlet with a couple TV commercials and bit parts for a resume - signed on this project as one of the supporting cast at her uncle's request.

"No, he's not related to anyone. He actually works in a restaurant down in Malibu."

"A waiter?" she said, trying to limit the exasperation in her voice. "You've got to be kidding me. Singh will never go for an inexperienced unknown for the male lead."

Singh was the director assigned to the movie project.

"We know that it's going to be a hard sell, but just do us a favor and go look at the kid," Pauline said. "Dinner is on us."

"How did you find this guy?"

"It's an interesting little story, but before I tell you, I want your evaluation. Doable or not doable? You know that I respect your opinion."

Pauline knew how to get what she wanted from people.

"It's probably not doable. You know these things just don't happen," Carol said. "How will I know if I'm looking at the right guy?"

"His name is Thomas, and I think you'll know."

This had better be good, Carol thought to herself after she hung up the phone. The vampire movie was Pauline's baby, so she could not try to blow her off.

This project was a big one for A. M. Casting, already taking a lot of her staffs' time. They had spent a bundle of time and money on videotaping and were ready to start doing callbacks for the male leads; so, she would take a good look at the guy, as requested, and give her professional opinion to Pauline. Chalking it up as part of

the job, she rescheduled her day to allow for a late
afternoon trip to Malibu.

4

Casting Audition with an Agent to Go

Carol Berman had no trouble finding Bluestones Restaurant on Pacific Coast Highway in Malibu. She had eaten here before, but it was some time ago. The restaurant was on the beach and known for good food. Windows in the dining area looked out onto the Pacific shore and western horizon. There was nothing not to like about the place *if* you could get a table, which discreetly favored the wealthy Malibu crowd.

It was four-thirty when she walked through the wooden, double doors. The restaurant was quiet, and her eyes made the adjustment to the low lighting after being in the bright sunlight. There were a few people here and there in the background gearing up for the dinner crowd.

A good looking, young man in a dress shirt and tie stood by the podium in the entrance foyer, talking with a well-dressed woman emitting an air of authority. They both turned to face her.

Carol noticed the name 'Thomas' on the young man's tag pinned to his left breast pocket. His heavily lashed, dark eyes met hers directly and he smiled at her.

"Are you here for an early dinner?" he asked politely.

She nodded.

"Will there be anyone else joining you?"

Carol couldn't seem to look away from his eyes, which were dark blue with iridescent shards.

"No, I'm here by myself," she answered. "I didn't have time for lunch."

The host was definitely photogenic, she thought to herself. He was attractive in an alluring way, but didn't quite have the Hollywood look of most of the glossy pictures currently sitting on her desk back at the office.

Thomas picked up a blue, leather menu and led the way into the eating area of the restaurant. He had a small window table in the corner that he usually saved for his occasional single guest, or couples that were into themselves.

Carol followed behind and sized him up to be a little over six feet tall. He was wiry thin with wide shoulders. He didn't walk like a dancer but maneuvered gracefully along the aisle between the rows of tables. He came to a small table, pulled out the chair and waited for her to be seated. Taking in the ocean view, she realized that he had seated her at a prime table.

Thomas leaned toward her handing her the menu.

"On Special, we have a lobster bisque with breadsticks, or a salmon and asparagus salad if you would like something chilled," he mentioned. "Can I get you something to drink or a glass of wine?"

She gazed up at him, with the light from the window hitting his face. His skin was off-white and flawless, which contrasted with his short, dark brown hair and midnight blue eyes. Dark lashes and gray shadows accented his eyes. The nose was straight, and his cheekbones were high. He was closely shaven, but did not seem to have much facial hair. His mouth was wide and animated when he spoke. His lips were smooth and pale. Then she realized that he was waiting for an answer to a question.

"Oh, the wine. Yes, a glass of the house white will be fine."

"Your waitress will be Julie, and she will be here in a minute," he said, and turned to leave.

I don't want Julie, she thought to herself as he walked away. Carol had to admit Pauline was dead on. This kid was a ringer. He was a find as rare as a dragon's egg. He had the face, eyes, voice, charm, body, and agility all in one package. Now, she wanted to know Pauline's story and how she found him.

Mrs. Rielly sat on a high stool behind the bar where she could canvas the restaurant. It was a favorite spot for her. She had been watching the single woman by the window with interest since she came in. She was not tall. Silver gray stands of hair attractively mixed with the black, denoted her middle-age. Her clothing was casual with a short-sleeved, silk blouse and tailored lavender pants. High end department store fare, Mrs. Rielly surmised.

The restaurant owner didn't recognize the woman, but she instinctively knew that she was here for a reason. Rather than spending most of her time gazing out at the spectacular view of the beach, the woman seemed to be scrutinizing the restaurant, and especially watching Thomas whenever he came into the eating area. When she thought that the woman would be preparing to leave Mrs. Rielly moved to the foyer where Thomas was standing.

Carol paid the check, leaving a nice tip for Julie, an efficient waitress. She took a last look at the ocean view as she pulled a business card out of her purse. This should be interesting, she thought to herself as she walked toward the restaurant entrance.

Thomas was having a low conversation with a waitress. Carol went to stand next to him and interrupted.

"Excuse me," she said. "Could I have a word with you?"

The waitress faded away.

Thomas looked at the attractive guest, hoping that she didn't have a complaint about the food or the service.

"I would like to introduce myself. I'm Carol Berman,"

she said, holding her business card in her left hand. "I am the owner of an entertainment casting agency. I'm currently working with Checkmate Studios, casting for a movie with Briana Stillwood."

She held out her right hand, and was a little unnerved by the cool, light grip of Thomas's fingers on hers.

"I think you may have the look for one of the parts that we're currently casting."

Thomas was really taken off guard. The woman's words were rumbling together in his head: casting… Briana… part. The round face was looking up at him with dark, brown eyes.

"Do you mind if I ask you a couple questions?" she asked.

He didn't answer, but looked at her with a look of assent, waiting for the question.

"Can I ask how old you are?"

"Twenty-one," he answered.

At least, that was what his California driver's license reported.

"Have you ever had any acting experience?" she continued her query.

This was not an unusual question since half of the aspiring actors in Hollywood worked part-time jobs, in restaurants and bars, to leave daytime hours open for casting calls and auditions.

"No, I've never done any kind of acting," he answered.

In fact, this was the only decent job he ever had, he thought to himself.

"Would you consider coming to our office in Glendale on Monday? I would like to take a few pictures, and maybe have you read something during a videotaping."

Carol tried to play down the purpose of the meeting as she handed him her business card. She didn't want to scare him off.

Thomas stared at the card. It looked real enough, and she seemed to be on the level.

"Ah, yeah, I guess I could."

"Good," she said, smiling a half smile. "Between nine and ten?"

He nodded.

Then registering the anxious look on the young man's face, "Don't worry, it will be fine," she said, trying to be reassuring. "You can just wear jeans and a shirt. We have any extra clothes that we may want you to wear for pictures."

He continued to look at her not knowing what to say.

"Now, you won't stand me up, will you? Our office is right off the 5 Freeway. Exit at Alameda and turn right on Flower Street."

"Okay," he managed to get out.

Thomas was standing still, looking at the intricate, oriental design on the back of the woman's blouse as she walked out the door. Mrs. Rielly came over and took the stylish business card from his hand, reading the name and logo on the front of the card.

She shook her head.

Damn, she thought to herself. She was going to lose her handsome host.

* * *

On Monday, after missing the Flower Street turn, Thomas backtracked and turned onto the street. The morning sunlight hit the windshield. He automatically flipped the extra layer of sunglasses onto the existing frames that he wore. Another sunny day in Southern California, he groaned to himself. He was driving slowly through the semi-industrial, mainly non-residential neighborhood, trying to find the address. One after another small, one and two-story buildings lined the street.

Suddenly, black letters reading "A. M. Casting" on a gray, one-story building caught his eye on the other side of the street. There was a narrow, concrete driveway leading to the back of the building, where he found almost all of the available parking spaces filled.

The building looked small from the front, but the lot was deep, and the building had a long, rectangular shape. The front of the building was a façade, with the actual business entrance at the back through two heavy glass doors.

Thomas entered and walked to the waist-high counter in the reception area. He gave his name to the receptionist who told him to take a seat in the chairs lining the wall by the door. Shortly, a young, Asian lady led him to the interior of the office, through a maze of cubicles. He followed her down a hallway, and into a small room with a large chair in front of a mirror, which took up most of one wall. Clothes racks lined another wall. He soon learned that the girl's name was Wendy, and she explained that she would get him ready to be photographed.

She handed him a long-sleeved, gold-colored shirt and a lightweight, black jacket. Wendy did not leave or turn around as he changed shirts, so he tucked the new shirt into his jeans as best he could without unzipping his pants. As he put on the jacket, she pointed toward the chair.

Once he was seated, Wendy rubbed some styling gel between her palms and worked it into his hair. Using only her hands, she styled his short hair into a disheveled style. Then she pulled out a large tray containing various kinds of makeup. It reminded Thomas of the second drawer in his mother's bathroom which was full of half-used, drug store makeup. The girl quickly applied a foundation to his face, used a pencil to better define his eyebrows, and put a matte, coral color to his lips, which she blended evenly. She used just a touch of mascara on his lashes saying that he really didn't need much of that. Regarding the final effect, Thomas was surprised at the change a little hair gel and makeup could make.

Next, Thomas was led down a narrow hallway that opened into a large room. The space was cluttered with many items that didn't seem to go together. There were several back screens of different colors, lighting stands of various types, chairs, pots with oversized plants and a few artificial trees. Wendy handed Thomas off to a blonde, spiky-haired guy named Art, who was busy working with a camera on a tripod.

"Okay, first I would like to try a few shots over here by this tree," Art indicated a set off to one side.

The background scene was obviously a night sky of multiple shades of grays, depicting clouds, and a crescent moon. The so-called tree was actually a prop, with a gnarly trunk and bare, twisted branches. Art came over and positioned him, standing slightly sideways, one hand perched on a lower limb of the fake tree, and told him to look toward the camera. Art asked him questions as he worked, eliciting changes of expressions on Thomas' face as the camera clicked in quick succession, taking one shot after another. Art continued to give Thomas directions for changes in positions and poses. He then had Thomas remove the jacket and open one button on the shirt, before taking another set of pictures.

"Okay, take a break," Art said, who stopped to fiddle with the camera and light stands.

Thomas found a folding chair sitting nearby and sat down. He wondered how long this was going to take and if he would see the woman from the restaurant that asked him to come here today.

Thomas was not sure what made him notice the change of atmosphere that suddenly came over the place. There was a hum in the air. Thomas sensed a quiet excitement in the staff milling through the cavernous room. More people had appeared on the other side of the space, seeming to materialize from nowhere, quietly whispering to one another in pairs or small groups.

From the back of the room, Carol Berman, accompanied by a tall, thin woman, approached Thomas. He stood up as they came toward him.

"Thomas, good to see you. I'm so glad that you could make it this morning. Did you have any trouble finding the place?" Carol asked.

"Ah, no," that was all that he could seem to muster at the moment.

"I'd like you to meet Joey Madison. Joey is Briana Stillwood's manager," said Carol.

"Nice to meet you," said Thomas, while gently grasping the woman's extended hand.

She smiled at him in a closed-lipped smile of

acknowledgment.

Carol turned to Joey and said, "Come on into my office and have a latte with me, while we let Art do his magic."

Carol and Joey walked away toward the front of the building. Thomas, feeling dismissed, sat back down in the folding chair, waiting for Art who had wandered off somewhere. Maybe they were done with him, he thought.

Wendy appeared from the makeup area, but Thomas barely noticed her due to the person at her side – Briana Stillwood.

Thomas couldn't help but stare. Her thick, blonde hair had been intricately braided, revealing her wide forehead, and accentuating her perfect eyebrows and large, sea-green eyes. Her mouth and cheekbones were a shade of pink. She wore a maroon, long-sleeved blouse with offset buttons and a flap below her neck, which revealed the hollow at her throat. Briana had been poured into a pair of skin-tight, black pants that hugged her legs to the tops of black, leather boots. Thomas stood up as they walked toward him.

"Briana this is Thomas. Thomas, this is Briana," said Wendy.

"Have fun," she smiled as she exited, stage left.

Thomas managed a weak, "Hi."

Briana was fighting to control her emotions, and to keep her expression blank while her heart pounded. Had a good fairy heard her plea to see this guy again, she wondered? Did someone know that she had driven by the Malibu restaurant twice, never having the courage to go in? He looked different. Maybe it was the hair, but the enticing eyes were the same.

"Hi," she managed. "I remember you from the

restaurant in Malibu. You work there."

"Yes," said Thomas. "I remember when you came in."

The magical Art appeared and interrupted the conversation that had barely begun.

"Okay, let's do this!" he said.

The next forty minutes flew by as Art posed the awkward couple in one almost-intimate pose after another, his trusty camera clicking away.

Thomas and Briana gradually relaxed and warmed to each other. They were able to follow directions when Art directed them to look at each other 'with longing'. Slowly, true feelings exposed themselves on their faces - both lonely and wanting - and Art caught the shots.

Lastly, they stood beside the fake, gnarly tree before the scenic background. Briana stood in front of Thomas with her back leaning against him, his arm bent across her upper chest in a possessive grasp, both looking straight ahead at the camera

Carol and Joey had quietly come to stand behind the talented photographer. The contrast between the fair Briana and the dark-haired novice was striking. Both women could see the making of a large movie poster, ready to line the walls of movie theaters.

"Wow," Carol said, beneath her breath.

Pauline had called this one right, she thought to herself. Now, can he read?

"Francie," she yelled for her assistant.

When the girl appeared, "Get me one of those sides we were using to film the male leads the other day. Art, set up for a videotaping. Mel, make a small restaurant scene using that background over there, and a small table with two chairs. Maggie, find two coffee mugs with water in them, and a potted candle for the table. Let's go people!"

"What are sides?" Thomas whispered to Briana.

"Oh, it's part of a script. They're going to have us read a little bit of a scene to see how we look together," explained Briana. "They're going to videotape us."

Thomas nodded as if he understood what she was saying – like he did this all the time. The 'side' turned out to be one page of dialog printed on pink paper between the male and female characters.

"Let's read through this together while they're getting ready," suggested Briana. "When we do the scene in front of the camera, just keep eye contact with me and don't look at the camera. Do your best to get the gist of the dialog – it doesn't have to be perfect. We can support each other."

As much as he was trying not to, Thomas felt a major panic attack coming on. If he was able to sweat, he would. If his mouth wasn't already dry, it would be drier. Wendy appeared with a change of jacket, and a touchup of makeup for both him and Briana. Thomas read through the scene. His character was explaining to Briana's character his need to leave and never see her again, even though he would never forget her. Thomas didn't know his character, but he knew that he *did* want to see Briana again. It was not hard to pretend that he would grieve over her loss.

On Art's command, they started the scene with the camera recording. The first attempt didn't go very well, with too many long pauses in the dialog. The second attempt went better, with Thomas matching Briana in keeping the scene going - until the end.

Trying to look casual, Thomas picked up the cup before

him, holding it as he spoke his line, *"We can't be seen together, it's too dangerous for you."*

However, he was holding his forearm over the candle. Briana watched with horror as the cuff of his shirt caught fire. Thomas continued with his dialog, not appearing to notice the sleeve catching fire. Briana grabbed her cup of water and threw it over the fire, which didn't completely extinguish it. She then grabbed the cup from Thomas's hand and poured its contents over the sleeve and candle.

The audience behind the camera, which had grown to a crowd, gasped and 'owed' in unison, and then fell into silence.

"That's good, Art. I think we have enough," said Carol.

Dismissing the onlookers, she added, "Doesn't anyone have anything to do around here?"

"Are you all right?" Briana asked Thomas.

Thomas examined his now wet sleeve and arm and realized what had happened. He hadn't felt the flames against his skin.

"I'm okay," he said. "I guess I ruined the scene."

"No, I don't think so. We were almost finished anyway," she said, supportively.

"I'm sorry. I've never done this before," Thomas said, continuing to examine his arm.

At this point, the superwoman Wendy swooped over to the table with a first aid kit and began searching for a bandage for the affected arm. As Wendy finished, Francie came to the small table.

"Ms. C wants to see you in her office. Follow me," she said to Thomas.

Thomas stood up and said looking at Briana, "Well, I probably won't see you again, so it was nice to meet you."

"It was nice meeting you, too," said Briana.

"I hope you get the part," she added, as he was walking away in Francie's wake.

The path to Carol Berman's office was a virtual maze that led to the executive office at the front of the building. On the way, Thomas rehearsed a speech for being told that he didn't get the part. Francie ushered him into the large, petitioned, executive office.

Carol was on the office phone but signaled for Thomas to sit down in one of the fiberglass chairs positioned in front of the clear, glass slab with steel legs being used as a desk.

"How did you like meeting Briana?" Carol asked Thomas, after she put the phone down.

"It was good to meet her."

"Would you like to work with her in a movie?"

"I'm not sure if I could do it. I don't think I did very well today."

"For someone that has no experience and has never done this before, you did well. I'll just have to package everything properly to sell you to the director. He can be abrasive at times, but he puts out a good product in the end."

"You're not telling me to leave?"

"No," she said, twisting her diamond ring to its correct position on her ring finger. "I was wondering if you had more time today to go meet another person. I need to get you signed up with an agent. I'm going to give you her address. She's located in Studio City."

"Yeah, I have time. I don't need to be at *Bluestones* until five o'clock," he said, thinking out loud.

"That's another thing," Carol said, running her right hand through her hair, "If you get this part in the movie, you would have to quit that job. This would be more than full time over the next six months. Are you up for that?"

Carol noticed some hesitation before Thomas said, "Yeah, I'm cool with that."

Thomas knew that his life was taking a turn. His hesitation wasn't about losing his job at Bluestones. His hesitation was about surviving as a vampire in Hollywood without being discovered.

* * *

Two hours later, Thomas found himself sitting in a small, cluttered office on the second story of an office building - with no parking - on a main street in Studio City. A plump, short-haired woman with a round face, sat behind the desk with her attention moving between the computer monitor and the cell phone she was using. Thomas had heard that Hollywood was run by men, but so far, he was beginning to think that women did all the work. Carol Berman sent him to meet with Maggie Finchlock. Maggie was a theatrical agent that represented film and television actors.

The meeting started with the little firehouse of a woman firing questions that came in quick succession, most of which ended with the answer of 'no' from Thomas. She quickly discerned that she had her work cut out for her by representing someone with absolutely no IMDb - Internet Movie Database – credits, which actors attained as they worked on various projects. Carol would owe her for this one.

Maggie spent the next ten minutes explaining the agent-actor relationship, how she was going to help him get some work prior to starting on the movie, so that he would have a little experience before the camera. She explained the unions, the usual pay scales, and how he paid for her services. Then she got busy on the computer and made several phone calls, using first names and calling in some favors.

As she worked, Thomas looked around the office and noticing the pictures on the bookshelf next to the desk. There was a picture of a bride and groom, and one of a baby sitting on a rug behind letters spelling 'one'. Possibly the agent's family, he thought, as the woman talked into the phone. Suddenly, the call ended, and her full attention turned to Thomas.

"Okay," she said, with satisfaction. "I was able to get you a speaking part in an orange juice commercial that's shooting on Tuesday. It will give you your first IMDb credit to get you started. Here is the address of the orchard up in Ojai where they're filming. Be there at eight in the morning and don't be late. Ask for Richard when you get there."

Maggie tore a sheet of paper from the tablet and handed it to Thomas across the desk, "Can you do that?"

"Yeah, sure. Thanks," Thomas said in a daze, wondering what he was getting into.

"I'll call you when I hear anything about the vampire movie. Carol sounded pretty confident, but they still need to get the director on board. This is an amazing shot for you, Thomas. I hope you appreciate that," she said, looking at him with notice.

"By the way, don't cut your hair. You'll need it to grow out a little."

At this point, the phone rang. Maggie waved him off as her attention went to the call at hand.

Walking to his car - parked three blocks away - the changes of the day weighed on Thomas. He hated to give up his job at the restaurant. He wondered if he would be making enough money if he got the part in the movie. At least Bluestones was a steady job.

Then his thoughts went to Briana.

Damn, she was hot!

He loved being near her, smelling her hair and touching her hand. He reached into his pocket and found a lemon candy, popped it into his mouth and moved his tongue around it, letting the sour flavor do its work. The sun was beating on his back. He needed to get some blood.

5

Getting the Part

"You're awfully quiet," Joey commented to Briana.

She was sitting next to her in the front seat of the silver Mercedes on the way home from the casting office.

"I'm okay," replied Briana, with a sideways smile at her aunt who was driving.

Briana reached out and changed the radio channel from the talk station to one with music. In reality, she was still shaken inside and didn't want to talk about it with her aunt.

In the past two weeks, she had wrapped up her work on the TV show and signed the contract with Checkmate Studios for her first, full-length movie. She had met with the directors, and the pre-production schedule was provided. Things were moving fast.

Today she was blindsided at the casting office, finding Thomas there. Her aunt told her that the reason for the trip was to discuss some of the male actors that were in the running for the lead in the vampire movie, and possibly take some photos. Never in her wildest dreams did she expect to see the guy from the restaurant, who had been showing up in her thoughts just before going to sleep at night. She didn't even know his name.

"You can't deny it, you like him," the wise aunt said, glancing at her niece.

"I was just really surprised to see him. What was he doing there? He's not an actor. Did you know about this before we went? What's the deal?" Briana said, putting her aunt on the spot.

"Yes, I knew that he was going to be there. Carol had called me and given me a heads-up. She thought Pauline

Mellick was nuts when she first asked her to bring Thomas in; but today, after seeing how good you two looked together, I'm thinking that maybe she's not so crazy."

"Well, he does seem nice," said Briana, her voice softening, "but he has absolutely no experience, so I don't think there's much chance of him getting the part. He was so nervous doing his lines that he didn't even notice that his shirt was on fire. Look at the objections that Singh had about *me* not having any movie experience."

"The only one I'm worried about is you and your ability to get a successful movie out there. The script looks good, and the contract looks better. If this goes well, Checkmate Studios may have more good roles for you as a leading star," Joey emphasized.

"Let Pauline deal with Singh. She knows how to get what she wants, and it looks like she's set on *that* young man."

The inside of the car fell silent. Briana let her thoughts wander at the possibility of Thomas actually getting the role opposite her in the movie. They would be thrown together for much of the film. In fact, many of the scenes would be just between the two of them. A rush of pink came to her face when she remembered some of the more intimate scenes in the script. She did seem to have a physical response when she saw him. She remembered leaning against Thomas for the pictures by the tree, and his arm holding her. His body had been hard behind her, and his arm strong. Lost in the moment, she felt totally protected from any stray vampires. She felt his breath on her ear, and she feared that he could feel her heart pounding.

At the little table, looking into his eyes, she used all of her self-discipline to remember her lines and help guide him through the scene.

For now, she would try to put all of this at the back of her mind. Let the bigwigs make the decision. Most likely she would end up being paired with a totally different, experienced actor in the lead role. She was leaving on a much-needed vacation to the Bahamas with her mother and father the next day, and she still wasn't packed.

* * *

The following Friday, Carol Berman and her assistant Francie were the first to arrive at Studio AB-6 toward the back of the busy studio lot in Burbank. Carol was carrying a cardboard box containing the casting files and presentation folders she had prepared for the meeting. The PowerPoint presentation provided statistics and several head shots of the last of the potential cast members for the vampire movie, now under the working title of *Vampire Lost*.

Francie went back out to the Suburban for the second of three, large posters that Carol had the art department create from Art's photos of Briana and Thomas standing by the tree. The artist was as able to add the title and a more dramatic background effect, highlighting the appealing, sexy duo.

"Put that one over there by the door so they can see it when they walk in," Carol directed Francie. "And then one on each side of this railing, facing the rows of seats."

This was a small studio with only fifty seats, broken up into three uneven rows, facing a large screen. It was primarily used by directors to show dailies – or review film taken during a day of shooting. The purpose of this meeting was to finalize the casting selections for the supporting cast, and male lead actor, to work with Briana Stillwood. The *real* reason for the meeting was to convince a sometimes-petulant director to accept an untrained, inexperienced actor for the lead role opposite Briana.

Art arrived with his computer, and other equipment, and started setting up. He knew the drill. Carol's team had spent the week editing and re-editing the presentation, leaving all of the shots and video of Thomas and Briana to be shown last.

Sadamandi Singh was the next to show up at the small studio. He wore his trademark turban, had a long, thin beard, and sported a traditional muslin tunic over jeans. Singh was a Sikh who had minimally adjusted to the American culture since moving from Bombay, India twelve years previously. His reputation for directing flashy Bollywood movies, sometimes managing large casts of extras, and difficult scenic locations had proceeded him to Hollywood. Checkmate Studios, in its initial throws of producing full-length features, snatched him up at a reasonable salary, which increased through the years. Singh gained the respect of Adam Siegal and Pauline Mellick for bringing projects in on time and usually within budget. His expertise with lighting effects would add drama and suspense to a film with the many night scenes called for in the vampire movie script.

Behind Singh, trailing into the theater was his cohort, assistant director Alicia Perry. She had worked with Singh on three projects and specialized in choreographing and filming action scenes. She had started in the film industry as an athletic stuntwoman fifteen years ago, and still trained stunt actors in a side business when she was not working on a film. She took a seat in the front row next to Singh. She was tall, thin, and wearing her usual shirt and jeans. Alicia had a hard look about her with an angular face and a short, blonde hairstyle which left the left side of her head shaved close. One could not help but notice the colorful tattoos covering her arms below her short shirt sleeves. This was one 'no bullshit' female.

"Let's get going here," Singh demanded, as Carol handed him a folder.

"We're ready to start, but Pauline wanted to be here," Carol explained.

"Then she should have been on time," Singh retorted.

"How many do we have here?" he asked, starting to leaf through the paperwork.

"We can start with some of the supporting cast prospects. Alicia, you may want to look at the resumes we've prepared for our two villainous vampires. All of them have either done some stunt work or action scenes."

Carol gave Art the signal and he began projecting the head shots and videotaping onto the large screen. Carol introduced each actor and gave highlights of their experience. Singh must have wanted to get home early because the presentation went along at a fast pace, moving from one actor to the next without many interruptions.

Singh and Alicia put their heads together, quietly discussing each prospect. An actor and a backup was selected for each role of villain vampires. The roles of parents for Briana's character needed to be selected and were recommended from a group of older character actors. Singh was happy with Carol's suggestions. Two actresses were also chosen to play school friends of Brianna's character, one of which was Jennifer Weingart, Adam Siegal's niece. The role was not a large one, and Singh was alright with her getting the part. She had some commercial experience.

Suddenly, the door opened at the back to the darkened studio, and the afternoon light flooded onto the wide screen in front of the rows of seats. Pauline Mellick stepped into the room, quickly removing her sunglasses.

She was followed by the tall figure of Adam Siegal, the man himself. Together they walked down a slight incline to the front row of seats, both greeting the two directors. They took seats next to the pair. Singh and Alicia were surprised to see Adam, which was very unusual for a casting session.

"We're sorry we're late. Where are we at?" asked Pauline, as she took the file Carol handed her.

Carol quickly went through the file, pointing out the selected actors and actresses, bringing Adam and Pauline up to speed.

"We've narrowed the male lead role opposite Briana - our *good* vampire - to three actors, if you can turn to the green tab in your folder," Carol directed.

The first, young, blonde actor was presented, his experience discussed, and several in-costume photographs were displayed. Two videos were viewed. Alicia was supportive, but Singh didn't feel the connection with Briana, commenting that he was too good-looking and there was no contrast between the two young people.

The second actor was the most experienced and also had a television show under his belt. He was well known with some fan following and could add to the buzz for the film in the marketing process. He would require a higher paycheck and stretch the budget. His looks were dark with black hair, a full-jawed, handsome face with heavily lashed, brown eyes. He showed well on video and breezed through his lines. The casting agency shot two scenes with Briana, which were stunted. The chemistry was clearly not there. Briana's body language leaned away from the guy, and there was hardly any eye contact between the two.

"Next, we have Thomas Johnson. He's new to the business, so we could probably pay him at union scale with an introduction credit," said Carol, pointing out a positive.

As Carol spoke, Art was flashing still pictures of Thomas on the screen, and then shots of Thomas and Briana.

"Where's his experience?" asked Singh. "There's nothing here," indicating the bio page.

"There are a lot of action scenes in this script. I was hoping for someone more athletic. This guy looks too thin. How's he going to look fighting with these other two guys we picked?" asked Alicia.

"Thomas is athletic. He's a runner, which explains his thin physique. Let's look at some video with Thomas and Briana," said Carol.

Art ran the video.

The two, young people read through the scene, unaware of other people in the world. They were believable as a couple. They were photogenic together. The scene ended with Briana putting out the fire on Thomas' shirt sleeve. Carol had decided to leave it in the cut, hoping to heighten the drama between the pair.

"God," Alicia said, with a gasp, when it was over.

"Play it again," demanded Adam. "I want a closer look at this guy."

Adam had the memory of a locked safe, and he remembered Thomas from the intimate wine glass scene with Briana in the Malibu restaurant.

Art replayed the video, and all was quiet when it was finished.

"A. M. Casting is recommending this young man for the part. The chemistry between these two is palpable. This is not just an action movie, but a love story."

"I can't believe that you want me to use an inexperienced actor in a lead role," Singh said, with disbelief.

"He does have a pallor about him. That second guy looks too healthy and tanned to be a vampire," Alicia interjected.

"We can get Thomas an acting coach," said Pauline.

"No," said Singh. "It's my movie, and I just can't have a novice in the lead! You're going to have to test some more actors."

As far as Singh was concerned the issue was closed.

"Look, Mandy," Adam said, using his familiar nickname for Singh. "I hear what you're saying. You and Alicia end up having to deal with the problems of working with Thomas once he's signed. This is your reputation, too," added Adam, commiserating with the director.

"Pauline and Carol seem to agree that this guy and Briana have a real attraction for each other; so, let's think of how we can make everyone happy. Let's get him an acting coach. Briana seems happy to work with him and can help carry him. We can extend the shooting schedule by two to three weeks and give you an extra five hundred thousand in the budget for possible retakes and other issues. How does that sound?"

The lights in the studio had been turned on after the last video. The quiet in the room was deafening as Singh considered Adam's proposal. Now he understood why Adam was here and realized that he had lost this argument before it began.

"All right. Sign the kid," said Singh, with a resigned sigh. "We'll do our best to make it work."

"Thanks, Mandy. Pauline and I really appreciate it," said Adam, reaching out his hand to shake with Singh.

Then pointing to the poster, "Carol, these posters look great. Make sure to get them to our marketing department to give them the idea."

***

When Carol got back to the office that Friday afternoon, she needed to get the ball rolling on the final casting selections for the vampire movie. She started making phone calls to the actor's agents, ticking off her list one by one. Last on the list was Thomas Johnson. His agent was Maggie Finchlock, someone that she had worked with from time to time over the years. They had a good rapport, which was why Carol had referred Thomas to her in the first place. She could handle people new to the business.

Carol thought back to the afternoon's meeting. Singh had come in, demanding and confident, and left understanding who held the purse strings. Pauline had gotten her way, thanks to Adam's long relationship with Singh and his negotiating skills. It was the first time in Carol's career as a casting director that she was able to place a non-actor in a lead role for a movie.

She made the call.

"Maggie, it's Carol Berman."

"Oh, hi Carol. What's up?"

"I'll be sending all of the paperwork over for Thomas Johnson. You can tell him that he got the part for the vampire movie with Briana Stillwood," Carol reported, getting straight to the point.

"You're kidding!" Maggie knew the director's reputation and was astonished by the news.

"Yeah. Pauline and Adam showed up at the casting meeting."

"Well, that's great news. I have to say that I've gotten to like Thomas. I've been sending him out on anything I can find, at least five days a week. So far, he's done an orange juice commercial and has a callback on a sunglass ad."

"It's the eyes…they're mesmerizing," Carol thought out loud.

"True, but I'm just trying to get him used to standing on a mark and reciting his lines. Also, he's been really dependable. I've gotten some good feedback even when he didn't get the parts."

"Oh, that reminds me. The deal with Singh required Thomas to get an acting coach. Try Handal's Agency. And try to get two-hour sessions with Handal himself, twice a week until Thomas leaves on location for the movie. The bill goes to Pauline Mellick at Checkmate Studios."

"Private sessions with Handal are expensive," Maggie retorted.

"That's good. Singh will be impressed. Get all the paperwork back to me as soon as you can. The studio is in pre-production now, and the first reading is the Monday after next."

"Will do. I'll keep you posted."

"Thanks, Maggie."

Carol hung up satisfied. It had been a hectic, but memorable day. She would reward herself and take the weekend off.

* * *

Thomas had just gotten home after an unsuccessful night trying to get blood from a couple of hospitals he visited regularly. It seems that there was a blood shortage in town and the hospital stores were down to the minimum. Today, he would visit a blood bank to buy some outdated units from a young lab technician he had befriended. It was a last resort, since the cost would drain most of his cash on hand, but that would have to do for now.

"Thomas, that woman called again and said you needed to call her back right away," his mother said, as she came into the living room from the back of the house.

"She called twice last night."

"Did she say what she wanted?"

Thomas had also gotten two calls from Maggie Finchlock on his cell phone the previous evening but had deliberately not called her back. She had been sending him out on auditions every day and he wanted the weekend free. When he didn't call her back right away, Maggie would call at the house. Thomas knew that his first priority today was to get some blood. He was feeling weak, and everyone getting too close was looking like a quick meal. The sour lemon candies were just not doing it.

"She said something about getting a part in a vampire movie with some girl, Briana something. What is she talking about?" his mother asked.

"What?" Thomas said, jumping up from the sofa and

facing his mother.

"I don't know what it was about. She said that you needed to come in and sign some papers for the movie part. She said that she was your agent. What agent?"

"It's a long story, Mom. What did she say about the part in the movie?"

"She said you got the part."

Thomas slowly sat down on the sofa again, digesting the fact that he would actually be working on a movie with Briana Stillwood.

"Thomas, what is this all about?" Lynnette Johnson demanded of her son.

When he didn't answer she said, "Now, Thomas. What's going on?"

"Okay, Mom. Sit down."

After his mother sat down on the sofa, she grabbed the TV remote, turned off the TV and waited for her son to start his explanation.

"A few weeks ago, this lady came into the restaurant, had dinner, and on the way out asked me if I wanted to come to her work and take some pictures for a movie she was working on. She was trying to find actors. I told her that I wasn't an actor, but she said to come anyway. When I got to the casting agency, they took pictures and a video of me with Briana Stillwood. She's a TV star that's going to be in this movie. Anyway, they sent me to an agent for actors. That's who called. She's been sending me all over the place doing auditions for commercials and things. Are you sure she said that I got the part?"

"Yeah, that's what she said. So, let me get this straight. You're going to be an actor in a movie?"

"Sounds like it. I'll have to call her back."

The information was starting to sink in for Lynette Johnson.

"You're going to be in a movie? What kind of movie?"

"Well, I'm not exactly sure. It's some kind of vampire movie. I haven't read the script yet."

His mother laughed.

"My son the vampire," she said. "That's amazing."

"Look, Mom, don't get carried away. I need to find out more about this… and don't tell anyone."

"Okay, but it's so incredible. I can't believe that you're going to be in a movie."

"It's not a sure thing yet. Let me make sure it's for real, first."

"Are you all right, honey? You're looking kind of peaky. You're not getting sick, are you?"

"No, Mom. I'm just a little tired. I'm going to meet Josh for a hamburger. I'll come home and take a nap before I go to work. I'll try calling Maggie back later."

* * *

"Briana, I have some news on the movie," Joey said, walking out onto the patio where Briana was in a lounge chair next to the pool.

Briana put down the magazine and looked at her aunt.

"I don't believe it, but he got the part."

"What?" Briana asked, in disbelief.

"That guy from the restaurant got the lead role in the

movie. Carol just called me."

"Wow," Briana whispered.

While on vacation in the Caribbean, Briana tried to put Thomas - and the attraction to him - out of her mind. Only before going to sleep at night did thoughts of him seep in. To avoid disappointment, she prepared for the news of him not getting the movie role.

Now that he *did* get the part, she could think about seeing him again. Briana went into the house and up to her bedroom to seek privacy. Then, reading the movie script, she pictured herself with Thomas in the scenes.

Joey followed Briana back into the house. The wise aunt could see that the news of Thomas getting the acting job affected her niece. This was going to be a long summer, Joey thought.

* * *

It was Friday, and the last night Thomas would be working at Bluestones. He had given his notice a few days after being told he was getting the part in the movie with Briana Stillwood. On Monday, he had to be at the studio to read the script with the other cast members. It was really happening, and he was still trying to get his head around it.

The last time he had blood was Tuesday night, and he was thirsty again. Another reason for liking his job at Bluestones was that the beach was a natural attraction for girls.

Tuesday night after work, Thomas walked to the beachfront and found a dark-haired girl alone on the sand, staring out at the breakers. There was not much to see past the surf, due to the darkness and no moon in the sky. Thomas had to admit that he liked the girls. He hadn't gotten used to biting guys for blood. Girls were easier, cleaner, and didn't remind him of how he came to his fate of being a vampire.

"Hi," he said, sizing up her short, busty figure.

"Mind if I sit down?" he asked, in a most charming voice.

"Free beach," she said, continuing to stare out to sea.

"Are you from around here?" Thomas asked, after a long minute.

She turned and really looked at him for the first time. You would think that self-protective alarm bells would be going off in her head. Here she was alone, on a dark beach in the middle of the night, and a strange guy shows up.

"You were in the restaurant," she stated, in a factual way.

"Yeah, I work there," he said, in apologetic manner.

"You seemed very busy. I saw you go by a few times," she said.

A breeze came up and what little light there was hit the side of the girl's face and neck.

"I didn't see you," again apologetic.

"I was sitting in the bar. They have good apple martinis," she said, appreciatively.

Thomas could smell the alcohol wafting on her breath. She must have had a few drinks.

"Yeah, I know Bob, the bartender. He helped me get my job here."

Thomas paused strategically before continuing.

"So, are you from Malibu?" he repeated himself, trying to get more information.

"No," she paused. "I live in the Valley…with my so-called boyfriend."

Ah, Thomas thought to himself, the not very sober, damsel in distress - a specialty dish.

"Sounds like you might not want to go home," he said, in his most comforting voice.

She looked at his shadowed face, and into his sympathetic eyes.

"No, I want to stay here all night," she said, with a sigh. "Besides, I'm too drunk to drive back up Malibu Canyon."

"Sensible," he agreed.

He waited for her to go on, but she stared back out at the breaking waves.

"I like to come out here after my shift and unwind before I drive up Kanan."

Malibu Canyon and Kanan Road were common routes back to the San Fernando Valley from the Pacific coast. Both roads were full of hairpin curves that have sent more than one tipsy driver over the side into gaping canyons.

The girl laid down on the sand and turned her face toward Thomas. The smell of the ocean, and her scent, started to get to him; but he sat very still. She started talking about the boyfriend and he half listened, nodding his head at appropriate times. Her breathing became heated, and her chest moved up and down. He slowly moved toward her, going down on one elbow. The V- neck of her dress exposed pale skin. As she prattled on, he absently touched a stray strand of her hair. This caused her to move closer, facing him, her body turned toward him. This is almost too easy, he thought.

Thomas turned his full attention to her face, and after a

few moments of seeing the invitation in her eyes, he brushed her lips lightly with his long fingers. Her hand moved to his chest. He lightly kissed her lips and her cheek. She moaned and pulled him towards her. He kissed her deeply, hearing and feeling her heart pounding. Now the question was which vein? He did not want to leave too visible a mark or a bruise. He could feel his teeth coming to full position and knew he had to move quickly. He nuzzled her neck, and she moaned again.

Wait! He stopped abruptly. His tooth caught on metal! He felt the instant burn on his lip.

Damn, he hadn't noticed the silver hoop earrings she wore. He had an immediate reaction to silver. He guessed this girl didn't buy the cheap jewelry.

This was not going well, he thought, but his teeth were in place and the time was right. His head descended quickly as his teeth sunk into the soft flesh over the brachiocephalic vein. She let out a muffled scream, but his grip on her was sure. She could not move from his grasp. The rhythmic waves pounded onto the beach as he drank deeply, tasting the alcohol in her blood. Pulling back was always the problem. He didn't want to be a murderer, but he needed the blood for his existence. He forced himself to withdraw.

The girl was limp in his arms, passed out cold, but her heart was beating at a steady rate.

Now, Thomas had the usual problem. What do you do with the girl?

She was easy enough to carry, but it was awkward. The fluorescent hands on his watch showed that it was a little after three o'clock. He surveyed the empty beach and parking lot for any possible witnesses. Carefully avoiding the restaurant security cameras, he hauled her over his shoulder and carried her across the highway to his car and dumped her into the front seat.

It was a short trip down Pacific Coast Highway to Santa Monica, where he pulled into the parking lot of St. James Hospital.

He parked next to other cars and watched the doorway near the emergency room entrance. The place was deserted and quiet. With stealth speed, he hurried to the back door, carrying his victim, and sat her against the wall by the door. Then he was gone…and she would never remember who he was, only the sense of an illicit embrace with a stranger on the beach.

6

Location, Location

Tables were set up in a large U-shape at the front of the cavernous sound stage in preparation for the reading of the vampire movie script by the newly assembled cast members. Large story boards with brightly colored graphics, looking like giant pages from a comic book, were placed around the outside of the tables, behind the chairs. The back of each chair was labeled with a cast member's name.

Thomas had some delay at the Checkmate Studio gate when the guard could not initially find his name on the list for entrance and had to make a call. It had also taken him a while to find Sound Stage 12 in the complex of alleyways and buildings, which looked like warehouses, toward the back of the lot.

When he entered the large, open space he noticed several people already milling around a table of breakfast snacks and beverages.

Shortly, a woman with a clipboard arrived and asked people to collect their food and drinks and take their assigned places at the tables. Thomas was soon to learn that the woman was Alicia Perry, the assistant director on the movie. A single table was set up facing the semi-circle group, where the lady with the arm tattoos took a seat. A middle-aged man with a white turban arrived and took a seat next to the blonde.

People were migrating toward the chairs, finding their places. On the table in front of each chair was a bound, paper script with *Vampire Lost* in bold letters on the cover. Thomas found his chair at the middle of the semi-circle and sat down, noticing that the chair next to him was tagged for Briana. So far, she had not made an appearance. He grabbed a lemon candy from his jeans pocket and popped it into his mouth. Just the thought of her sitting next to him all day made him thirsty, but he was looking forward to seeing her again.

He sat quietly gazing around the tables realizing that these were the actors that he would be working with on the movie. Just as the director was calling the meeting to order, the soundstage door opened, and Briana entered and walked toward her place. Thomas later learned that the stylish woman that came in with her was the costume designer.

"Hi," she quietly said to Thomas, as she took her seat and pulled a copy of the script toward her.

Thomas had no time to reply as Singh introduced himself and asked everyone to go around the table, say their name, and give the name of the character they would be reading. Introductions started at the end on one side of the semi-circle of chairs, and Thomas learned that not all of the people were actors. The script writing team took up one table, and a man who took a seat next to Alicia was introduced as the stunt director. Thomas felt his throat closing as the introductions moved from person to person, coming closer to him. Finally, it was his turn.

"Thomas Johnson. I'm reading Penn," he said, in a soft voice. The character's name was Pendragon, but went by Penn.

"Speak up!" demanded Singh.

Thomas repeated what he said in a louder voice. All eyes in the room were upon him with obvious curiosity. Briana introduced herself quickly, not giving Singh another chance to interrupt.

The reading of the script commenced with each actor reading their part as it came up in the printed dialog. Stage directions to the actors, within the script, were read by one of the writers. Briana was in most of the scenes, and Thomas listened to the change of tone in her voice depending on the dialog. Other than the action scenes, almost all of the scenes for his character were with Briana. The room became very quiet when the several love scenes between the characters of Thomas and Briana were read.

There were many interruptions during the reading, and time was taken to review the story boards. Also, changes in dialog were being made by the writers. Sometimes what looked good on paper didn't sound believable when read out loud. Thomas was surprised that they were still doing the reading as lunchtime came and went.

Finally, Singh called for an hour-long lunch break. The morning food tables had been cleared and replaced   by some   lunchtime   faire   of salads   and sandwiches.

Thomas was saved from making small talk, or standing around, by the costume designer who came in with Briana earlier. At a fast pace, she hurried him off to her offices at the front of the studio lot. There she assaulted him with a tape measure, writing down each measurement before moving on to another body part. She mumbled to herself as she went, 'wide shoulders, thin waist'.

When finished, she took the time to show Thomas some of the costume designs that were in production for his character. If she only knew that *real* vampires wore jeans and t-shirts, Thomas thought on his walk back to the sound stage.

The reading of the script resumed after the break. Thomas was beginning to realize what a lead role *was* due to the amount of dialog assigned to his character. At one point, Singh interrupted mid-sentence while Thomas was reading.

"No, no, no!" He called from his seat, facing Thomas,

"Can't you tell that this character is desperate? You can't read it like that!"

Thomas was embarrassed, not knowing what to say to the director.

Moments of silence passed.

"Mr. Singh, this is the first time he's seen the script," said Briana, in a soft voice. "We'll have time to rehearse this before we're filming the scene."

The great warehouse of a room was so quiet Thomas could hear Briana's slightly accelerated breathing. He didn't know if he should just continue reading the script.

"I'm sure that you are right, Miss Stillwood," said Singh, somewhat contrite. "Pick up where you left off, Mr. Johnson. I'm sorry for the interruption."

Thomas continued reading. Score one for team Thomas and Briana.

It was after two o'clock in the afternoon when the reading came to an end. Thomas wanted a chance to speak with his co-star, but he was immediately approached by Alicia and the tall, muscular man with a shaved head.

"Thomas, I'm Alicia Perry, the assistant director. This is Dogman Booker, our stunt director for the movie."

Dogman held out his hand to Thomas, who met his intense grip with the same strength.

"Rory, Kurt, come over here!" Alicia called to the actors playing the other vampires in the movie.

As they walked over, Thomas noticed that both men were taller than him and were built like refugees from a 24-hour Healthpoint Gym.

Alicia continued, "You all need to be here at nine on

Wednesday to get ready for the stunt work. We're building a practice set on this sound stage, for now. We'll be using harnesses for some of the action scenes. You'll have to get used to them for the jumps and flying leaps in the fight scenes. For the rest of the week, Dogman will put you through the preparation. We start shooting up in Santa Maria next Monday. Any questions?"

If there were any questions no one would dare speak up. The hard lady nodded to Dogman and left.

They were dismissed like lint on black pants.

* * *

"How did it go?" asked Joey, as Briana came into her aunt's downstairs office and plunked herself down in the chair next to the desk.

"Long. Terrible," Briana answered.

"Why? What happened? Did Thomas show up?"

"Yes, he sat next to me during the reading. I thought he did pretty well."

"So, what was terrible about it?" Joey asked, turning her attention to Briana from her laptop computer.

"I think that it's going to be a hard road with Singh. He didn't seem to like Thomas very much. At one point, he yelled at him for the way he was reading a scene."

"Well, Singh is known for that," commented Joey.

"He embarrassed Thomas in front of everyone. I kind of spoke up and Singh *did* apologize. It put a damper on the whole day. It was like a kid being yelled at by the teacher in front of the whole class."

"I'm sure Thomas will get better with some practice. I

heard from Carol that they are getting him an acting coach; *and* I'm sure you'll be able to help him," she said, dismissing the drama from Briana.

"Let's go get something to eat."

* * *

Wednesday morning came sooner than Thomas thought it would. Days were passing quickly. He scored some blood from a nearby dialysis unit Tuesday afternoon, so he was refreshed for the time being. He arrived at the studio on time. The guard at the gate had his name on the list and waved him in. When he got to the sound stage, Kurt and Rory were already there.

Dogman Booker showed up from the back of the building and led them out the door to his Chevy Tahoe which was parked outside the door.

"Load 'em up, boys. We're going for a run."

The Tahoe took off at a breakneck speed before the passengers got their seatbelts secured. After a drive on the freeway, surface streets, and into what looked like a residential area, Dogman parked the truck at the bottom of the Runyon Canyon Trail.

"Pile out!" Dog instructed.

Thomas noticed the sign for the hiking trail, where individuals and couples finished with their hikes were exiting.

"Welcome to Runyon Canyon, boys. This is a two and a half mile hiking trail popular for its scenic views of the Los Angeles skyline," Dogman said, as he passed out plastic bottles of water to each man.

"The trail makes a loop. I'll wait for you here."

He pulled a stopwatch out of his pocket and clicked the button.

"Well, what are you waiting for?" he said, looking at the blank faces. "Get going!"

Thomas took off running with a fond remembrance of his old football coach. This was just the sort of thing his coach used to do. It was a clear, bright morning in L.A., and Thomas was thankful for his sunglasses. Up the trail he climbed at a fast pace, easily passing numerous, struggling hikers.

Much was to be seen along the trail. He zoomed in on some birds in the bushes, saw ground squirrels rummaging in the dirt, and passed a coyote sleeping in his daytime hidey-hole.

As much as he hated the bright sunlight, he realized that it had been a long time since he was out with nature during the daytime hours.

He took a slight detour to help a lady whose dog had pulled the leash out of his owner's hand. Thomas ran down a gully after the dog, caught the leash, and returned the wayward animal.

About twenty minutes into the hike Thomas knew he was nearing the end of the trail, so he stopped and sat down on a rock in a shaded spot. Rory and Kurt were nowhere in sight. He took a couple sips of the water to wet his mouth and poured the rest of it out onto a nearby wildflower.

In a few minutes, he thought that he let enough time go by and got back onto the trail, ambling along toward its end. He saw Dogman standing by the black vehicle holding his phone to his ear. Thomas saw the surprised look on the man's face as he approached the SUV. Booker looked at his stopwatch.

"Thirty minutes and you're not even winded? Are you a runner?" Dogman asked.

"I worked down in Malibu and used to run on the beach after work. Sometimes I hike in the hills around Camarillo."

Dogman smiled, "Running in the sand. Yep, that will do it. Good one, kid."

Dogman was glad to know that this guy was not going to be the wimp of an actor that he had feared upon first seeing Thomas and the young man's trim physique.

Fifteen minutes later Kurt and Rory made their way to the Tahoe. The effects of the exertion were evident on their flushed faces and spent gaits.

"Yeah, you ladies need to hit the treadmill if you're going to make it through the next two weeks," was all Dogman said, getting into the Tahoe's driver's seat.

That afternoon, Dogman brought out the harnesses. The three stunt doubles that would be working on the film showed up. They demonstrated how to put on the harness, how to jump from a fifteen-foot platform, and how to land the jump.

Thomas was intrigued. He knew that he had the ability to do long jumps, but never tried it in public due to a fear of being discovered as immortal. Once he got into the harness, he was able to enjoy the jumps. After a few tries he started leaping upward before making the required decent.

Watching his young, lead actor, Dogman was impressed. The guy was a born stuntman. He showed no fear. The next day the team would practice flying in the harnesses and he was looking forward to it. For now, the ex-Army Ranger went home smiling, ready for a beer.

* * *

"Are you sure you have everything that you're going to need?" Lynette Johnson asked, looking at the duffle bag that her son had packed and left sitting by the front door.

"Yeah, Mom," replied Thomas. "They give you the clothes that you wear on the set, so I only need clothes for when I'm not working."

"What about food? You know how picky you are," his mother continued, always worried about his so-called anorexia.

"Food, are you kidding? All they *do* is feed you! They set up these long tables loaded with food - breakfast, lunch, and I'm told even dinner if they're filming late," Thomas explained, trying to relieve her anxiety.

"I may have to buy dinner sometimes, but someone said that the hotel is nice and has a restaurant. I'll be fine, Mom," he said convincingly, pulling her toward him into a hug.

"What's the cooler for?" she asked, referencing a small, blue ice cooler.

"I'm not sure if the hotel rooms have refrigerators. I was taking it so I could have cool drinks in my room," Thomas lied.

His real motive was to use the cooler as a possible blood storage container.

"I gotta go, Mom. The check-in at the hotel is four o'clock."

Thomas shouldered the duffle bag, and picked up the cooler, his mother hanging onto the last few moments by walking him out to his car.

"Call me when you get there!" she called, waving as he drove away.

The afternoon drive up the California coast to Santa Maria was scenic and unremarkable, allowing Thomas to think about the next few weeks when he would actually be filming a movie. The past week had been spent training with Kurt, Rory, and the stunt doubles.

The stunt guys would be taking their place in scenes when the action was considered too precarious for the actors. These scenes included fire, cliff climbing, and high-altitude jumps. The actors were required to do a certain amount of stunt work for close-ups and to maintain the credibility of the characters. Thomas was determined to do as many of his own stunts as possible, enjoying the physical action.

One thing that he was not going to miss was the two-hour sessions with his acting coach, Ty Handal. Ty hadn't acted in a movie since the seventies, but ran an extremely lucrative acting studio, providing lessons to many of the star-struck actors that showed up in ongoing waves to the Hollywood scene. He hired known, experienced actors to run his workshops which went on for several weeks and cost thousands of dollars.

Hoping to get more ework forwarded his way from Checkmate Studios, he had poured all of his expertise into his tutoring of the young, handsome - but totally inexperienced - Thomas Johnson. He had Thomas reading pages of dialog taken from famous plays and movie roles. He sent Thomas home with lists of old movies that were to be watched and discussed at the following coaching session.

Grudgingly, Thomas had to admit that he learned a lot about reciting lines in a very short time, not to mention learning the names of many famous actors in Hollywood's Hall of Fame.

Lastly, during the drive, his mind moved to the one possibility that concerned him most – the fear of being discovered as a *real* vampire. It was always at the back of his mind. He wondered if the camera would somehow betray him, showing something of his true nature. Also, the problem of getting blood on a regular basis was going to be a stretch for him. He didn't know the area. He knew that Santa Maria was surrounded by rural farmland with agriculture and animal breeding, but he wasn't ready to be spending his late nights sucking on a cow's neck. He would have to take a day-to-day approach and trust his ability to be innovative in order to secretly maintain his diet.

* * *

Monday at noon, Thomas was sitting in a chair in the makeup trailer, waiting for Colin to finish Rory's makeup. Rory's long, black hair, and the effects of the makeup, provided the sinister effect needed for his character. Playing a vampire wasn't easy for Rory since he was such a laid-back, sweet guy.

The week's filming schedule was waiting for Thomas when he checked in at the hotel the previous day. There was little change from day to day. Mornings were scheduled for rehearsal, and afternoons for filming. Action scenes were highly choreographed and broken into sections. Three cameras filming from different angles were used for highest efficiency.

The first three days were at one location site, where an important fight scene was being filmed. Movie scenes weren't shot in order of appearance in the film, so today's filming would appear in the second half of the movie. On this first day of filming Alicia was directing with Dogman assisting.

Dismissing Rory, Colin turned to Thomas.

"Kathy sent this over from wardrobe. You missed it when you picked up your outfit. You're supposed to be wearing it in all the scenes," he said, handing a disc- shaped amulet on a chain to Thomas.

The three-inch disc looked like metal, but Thomas could see that it was actually some kind of plastic or painted resin. The painted inlay of a dragon appeared on the front, and the attached chain was of wide, metal links. Thomas put the chain over his head and adjusted the amulet to hang in the center of his chest.

Colin began applying the foundation to Thomas's face and neck. The makeup had a luminous component, adding a slight luster to the skin that was already deathly pale.

"Man, you are the whitest dude I've ever worked on," Colin said, his own smiling, brown face looking into the mirror. "Don't you ever go out into the sun?"

"No, I kind of avoid the sun. I have a genetic skin disorder with low pigmentation. I get kind of flaky when I get sunburned."

Thomas wanted to establish a good vibe with Colin, since he would be doing his makeup every day. Thomas absentmindedly scratched at the skin on the back of his neck where the chain was now resting.

"That sucks, man. I haven't seen guys as white as you

since I moved out here from Michigan," Colin replied.

"Yeah?"

Thomas once again reached for his neck, disrupting the makeup artist. He noticed his skin starting to burn.

"Back where I'm from the sun doesn't come out for seven months out of the year. Lots of snow and overcast skies. I *love* this place! I'm never leaving California."

Thomas felt the skin of his neck start to sizzle. Realizing what was happening, he suddenly grabbed the neck chain and took it off over his head.

"Hey, man...what's happening?" Colin backed away, eyebrow pencil in hand. "You need to sit still while we do this."

"This chain is burning my neck," Thomas explained, throwing the offending object onto the table beneath the mirror. "I'm allergic to some metals, and this must be one of them."

Alicia Perry appeared at the open doorway of the makeup trailer.

"Colin, you're holding us up. We're ready to go on the set. Get Thomas out here."

"We've got a little problem here, Alicia. Thomas can't wear this chain that was sent over from wardrobe," Colin diverted, holding it out to her.

Alicia came up the steps of the trailer and entered the restricted space.

"He has to wear it. It's an identifier for his character in the script. He wears it in all of his scenes. What do you mean he can't wear it?"

"I'm actually allergic to some kinds of metal," Thomas

spoke up, taking Colin's place in the line of fire.

"It was burning my neck."

Alicia moved in behind Thomas, motioning Colin out of the way. She pulled down the back collar of the white, muslin shirt Thomas was wearing. She saw a line of red welts running along the base of the neck where the chain had burnt the skin.

"This is the worst allergic reaction I've ever seen," Alicia said, noticing little, white blisters on the skin. "You just put this on?"

"Yeah, he just had it on for a minute," Colin interjected.

"Okay, we've got to get on the set and get going. We don't have time to go back to wardrobe," Alicia said, scanning the cluttered trailer for an answer to the dilemma.

Looking at Colin she ordered, "Take off your boot, mountain man, and give me that black, leather shoelace."

While Colin removed his boot and shoelace, Alicia removed the amulet from the silver chain. She quickly threaded the attached ring of the circular form onto the lace, tying a knot at the ends of the shoelace. She slipped the revised necklace into place, positioning the dragon disc on Thomas's chest.

"Thank you, Ms. Perry," Thomas said.

"You can call me Alicia, Thomas. There's an EMT on the set. Have him put some ointment on the back of your neck before we start shooting."

Then addressing Colin, "Get a move on. I'll give you five minutes!"

She left the trailer in haste, while answering her bothersome cell phone.

Damn, Thomas thought to himself. He hadn't thought that his extreme reaction to metal would be a problem. Since his change, he had learned to avoid anything silver - or silver coated - usually after being burnt. He should have known that the metal chain could burn him. He would need to be more cautious in the future.

* * *

It was Tuesday afternoon. De Rossi had gotten up a couple hours earlier, taken a shower, and lazed around his modern, loft-style apartment in NoHo - a prestigious neighborhood in North Hollywood. Now fully alert, he began his daily computer reading of all the entertainment blogs and sites. He looked for current events, such as the premiere for the latest Merrill Summer movie at the Fox Theater tonight, and any new buzz on movie and TV deals. Today's Hollywood deals were tomorrow's fodder for publicity shoots. DeRossi made it his business to always know what was going on. In *this* town, the smallest thing could turn into the biggest publicity item overnight.

He debated with himself about covering the premier. He hated the woman and her smug attitude, displaying the conceit of Hollywood's royalty. He knew that the TV entertainment shows would cover the event *en masse*, so photos of the aging star would not bring much - hardly worth the gasoline to drive over there.

While browsing, he came across an article put out by the Checkmate Studio Publicity Department. It said that filming had begun on the promised Briana Stillwood movie – a vampire themed thriller. The young star was currently filming on the studio lot and would be joining the rest of the crew on the Santa Maria location site shortly.

Most of the article was about Briana, providing salutes to her prior accomplishments. A paragraph was devoted to the well-respected, character actors who were co-starring as her parents in the film. Toward the bottom of the article was a mention of a Thomas Johnson, who would have his acting debut in the movie as Briana's love interest.

DeRossi stared at the headshot of the would-be actor, suddenly remembering where he had seen him before. It was the kid from the restaurant who had stopped him in his tracks as he was trying to get shots of Briana. DeRossi's antenna went up. This was bizarre. He would need to make a few calls to find out more. He could smell a scoop.

* * *

Thomas was in the harness, preparing for the leap off the staircase banister to the marble floor twenty feet below. His   character, Penn, was fleeing the two pursuing vampires quickly approaching up the wide, curved stairs.

This was the second day of filming in the two-story, 1930's art deco building in downtown, Santa Maria. The building, previously a bank, had just been purchased and was in the process of being refurbished into a restaurant featuring high-dollar cuisine.

In the meantime, the owners were happy to make a few bucks from renting the space to the studio for filming. The high, elongated windows on the second level allowed light to filter down onto the main floor. Carved columns, jutting upward, supported the second level that went around the central, open space that ended in a majestic dome at the top of the ceiling. The site was selected for its character, and a backdrop to the drama of the vampire pursuit called for in the movie script.

Cameras were rolling as Dogman gave Thomas the

signal to leap. Thomas was confident, having practiced the stunt several times that morning. He pushed off and his body flew out into the wide, open space.

Immediately he felt the harness jerk and he realized that he was in free-fall, zooming toward the floor below.

The sound of the young actor's body smacking onto the marble was stunning and sickening to all in attendance.

At once, mayhem erupted on the set while Dogman ran to the prostrate form lying on the cold, hard surface.

"Medic!" Dogman yelled, on his knees next to Thomas, examining him for signs of life.

"Call 9-1-1!" Alicia yelled out. "We need an ambulance!"

Alicia ran to the young actor, watching Dogman turn over the immobile form.

"Is he breathing?" she asked.

"Yeah, barely," Dogman replied.

He made room for the EMT who was already wrapping a blood pressure cuff around Thomas' limp arm, after checking for a pulse on his neck.

"I think I'm getting a pulse, but this damn thing isn't working. I'm not getting a blood pressure," the EMT said, as he was pumping the bulb to the machine for a second time.

"Get something to elevate his legs, and let's get him covered. He already feels cool, he's probably going into shock."

Cast and crew stood back as the three hovered over the motionless Thomas. An ambulance was on the way.

The minutes of waiting dragged on.

Thomas opened his eyes, coming to focus on the domed structure of the ceiling far above, only to be eclipsed by three frightened faces hovering close. It took a couple seconds for him to become alert, remembering the sudden fear that had shot through him as he fell.

Starting to move, he pushed the canvas tarp being used as a makeshift blanket off his body and tried to sit up.

"Whoa, kid," demanded Dogman, placing a restraining hand on Thomas's chest.

"You fell and hit the floor pretty hard. We have an ambulance on the way. Just stay still."

Thomas started taking inventory. His head hurt. His arms and legs seemed to be moving without a problem. His one shoulder and hip bone were sore as hell. He removed the blood pressure cuff from his arm and sat up.

"I think I'm okay. Just a little sore."

Dogman and the EMT stared at him in surprise.

"You have to go to the hospital and get checked out," Alicia stated.

Fear shot through Thomas. He didn't want to go to a hospital. He didn't want anyone with medical expertise to get close to him.

"No, I just need to go back to the hotel and get some rest," Thomas said, forcing himself into a standing position. "I'm okay. Just a little winded."

Rory and Kurt, standing on the sidelines, started clapping. Soon the room of cast and crew were also applauding Thomas, relieved that he was on his feet.

Thomas started pulling at the harness that was supposed

to support him during the jump.

"I must not have put this thing on right."

He unbuttoned his shirt and removed the harness.

"Let me see that harness," Dogman demanded, reaching for the appliance.

"Here's what happened," he said, holding the piece of canvas with a ring where the support wire attached to the vest. "This thing frayed off the vest! Where's Chad? This should have been noticed when the wire was hooked onto the ring!"

"It was fine this morning when I was jumping," Thomas said, as he heard the ambulance siren from outside. "It must have just come loose."

Paramedics poured in through the wide, double-doored entrance, equipment in hand. They came to an abrupt stop, their eyes scanning the room for their accident victim. Everyone was on their feet. Was this a false alarm? Alicia went to meet them.

"We had an accident while we were filming," she explained to the two wide-eyed responders, who were surprised by the large number of people at the scene. "One of our actors was doing a stunt jump from the top of the staircase when his harness broke and he fell to the floor."

"Did he lose consciousness?" asked one of the paramedics.

"Yes, he was unconscious for a few minutes and then came around," she answered. "We still want to have him checked out at the hospital."

"Where is he?" the paramedic asked, proceeding into the crowded room.

Alicia turned to the spot where she had last seen Thomas standing. Her mouth dropped open when she saw that he was gone.

Everyone focused on the spot, then looking around.

"Where did he go?!" asked the director, in a demanding tone.

Everyone had been watching the paramedics as they arrived, and no one had seen Thomas stealthily slip into the back of the building and quickly exit through a side door. He knew that he would have to answer questions later, but for now he was safe.

* * *

By the following week, everything on the location site changed. Briana Stillwood arrived on the set. Along with her came Singh, taking charge of the production. Along with Singh came a small city of crew members. The production included four camera crews, lighting and sound technicians, and many others that Thomas had no understanding of exactly what their jobs were.

Three Santa Maria hotels were being used to house everyone. One was for the directors, actors, writers, and some of the crew. Thomas was assigned to this hotel. Another hotel was for most of the crew, and the third for the overflow. This movie was bringing some real cash into the small, central coast town.

It was just before noon and the lunch break had commenced for all, except those crew members responsible for setting up the next scene. Singh was in a satisfied mood, signified by a lack of yelling, having completed two scenes that morning, which was rare in the slow-paced movie business. He was pleased with his star,

Briana, who was talented, prepared and professional. Singh also gave her credit for working with her novice of a co-star in rehearsing their scenes and giving him advice for some of the technical issues of being in front of the camera.

A small town of production trailers and trucks lined the parking lots and streets near the filming site. Briana and Thomas each had a trailer where they could hang out during some of the long pauses between scenes. For lunch, Singh always retired to his wife's trailer for his ethnically prepared vegetarian food. He demanded the studio provide two trailers for his use. One was for himself, and one was for his wife and mother, who always accompanied him on location. The makeup and wardrobe departments also had their own trailers. Additional trucks were loaded with lighting, sound and camera equipment.

Thomas sat in a chair by himself under a nearby shade tree, which overlooked all of the commotion on the set. From behind his extra-dark sunglasses, he could quietly observe all. The next scene, for which the set was being prepared, was just a modification of the previous scene. Stand-ins representing himself and Briana were on their marks, as technicians buzzed about them like bees. Alicia Perry paraded around the set supervising the action. Thomas noticed that she frequently ran her hand through her short, cropped hair as she gave directions to the staff.

Thomas saw Briana at the food tables making choices, sometimes hesitating over selections, and then moving on. He watched as she took her plate over to sit with Jennifer, who had some dialog in the earlier scene. He popped a lemon drop into his mouth as he thought of Briana and his desire to be near her, then thinking of his own unnatural hunger that made him stay to himself. It was hard to be around Briana who smelled so good, and whose jugular vein seemed to increase its pulsations when he was near.

He felt the attraction between them but had not pursued it. In fact, he had already earned a reputation as a loner on the set. He was polite, but usually alone when not working.

Singh arrived on the set wearing a scarlet turban and fresh white tunic. His presence sent the signal that the lunch break was over. He spoke to the camera crews. Two cameras would be filming simultaneously on the next scene. Even though it was daylight, a light bar that resembled a football goalpost was set up, the crossbar housing banks of spotlights of various shades directed toward the actors on the set. Lighting staff were tweaking them into exact positions.

Thomas quickly reviewed the green sheets with revised dialog lines for the next scene. There were not many changes for his character. He got up and walked toward the set and saw Briana doing the same. They went over the dialog together, while waiting for cameras and lighting to complete their preparations.

Makeup and hairstylists showed up with their last-minute touch-ups for the pair. Stand-ins were dismissed, and Briana and Thomas took their places on the marks. A hush fell over the set, indicating the crew was finished and the set was ready for filming.

Singh stood by the lead camera and gave the order for 'Action'. The scene marker clicked, and the cameras rolled.

Briana started with her lines and Thomas followed, both trying to put the correct inflections on the dialog as their characters interacted. Singh watched, finding no reason to interrupt. This was the first of at least three takes, so he let the scene follow its course.

Suddenly, Thomas saw movement in the periphery of his vision, the light bar falling toward them.

In a split second, he stepped forward toward Briana, grabbed her, and fell on top of her.

Fractions of a second later, he felt the full impact of the light bar hit him, landing across his back. Spotlights broke around them as they hit the ground. Crew members surged in, pulling the heavy lighting equipment away from Thomas and Briana.

They sat up gingerly, trying to avoid the shattered glass on the ground around them. Briana was shaken and leaned into Thomas's chest with a cry. Thomas automatically enclosed her in his arms. They sat together in the embrace as the havoc ensued around them. There would be no more filming today.

7

Show Stopper

The filming on the vampire movie had not gone well that day. Singh was uptight over the limited time for set-up, and filming at the school campus location. The weather was not helping with the sun peaking in and out between rain clouds. This was a do-it-today situation, as the campus was closed due to some manufactured holiday. This meant they had one day to set up and shoot four scenes, along with some background shots. Both camera crews were on site to get it all done. People were tripping over each other and the mood was tense.

Thomas was doing all right with the madness and irritability around him. He was inhaling the scent of Briana's hair, which hung in long, flaxen waves as she stood a little too close to him. He was trying to focus on his lines for the scene but was distracted by his co-star who was looking too good today in a tight, mini skirt. Her legs were long and tanned, he noted. Her white top clung to her girlish figure, soft and round.

Thomas forced himself to look at the script rewrite. He knew his lines and did a quick memorization of the changes, but his attention kept drifting. There was a small mole on Briana's neck below her left earlobe, and she smelled so good. He made himself change position and stand more erect. This was not rocket science, he thought. He could *do* this, but his mind wandered again. She wore pink lip gloss and a hint of green eye shadow.

Once filming began, Thomas had a problem hitting some of the physical marks during the first take. The camera angle was tight, and he had to be careful not to go out of range. Briana was shorter and he had to lean in just right. There were several retakes, but no more than usual. He loved being in a scene with Briana but had to admit that he was a little nervous.

Singh's perfectionism was in high gear as he felt this was an important scene to get right. Everyone was suffering under his scrutiny. The scene ended up being rewritten again on the spot but was finally completed.

Briana was endlessly patient and helped drag him through, casually pulling off whatever was asked of her. His admiration for her grew daily. This acting stuff was harder than it looked from where you sat at the movies. It was very technical. During one scene when they were supposed to be walking along a campus hallway with the sun coming in from the upper west side, he had stepped into her light casting a shadow over her face.

Singh went nuts, yelling 'Cut, cut!', while waving arms above his blue turban.

Consequently, they filmed the shot two more times.

"I'll have to take care of it in editing," Singh yelled, and stalked off in a huff to check the setup for the next shot.

It was a little awkward when the scene was finished. Thomas wanted to talk to Briana. Hell, he wanted to be alone with her, but there was no available privacy. Where were all of his good lines when she was around, he thought, sarcastically? What was up with his ability to enchant her when he needed it? It was Friday afternoon, and they were not filming again until Monday.

"So, what are you doing this weekend?" he asked, trying to sound casual.

What does a famous TV star do on weekends, anyway? He wondered. She was probably totally booked.

"Oh, I'll just hang out at home. I need to catch up on some things, and I'm kind of tired from getting up so early every day," she said, flicking her hand to remove stray hair from the side of her face. "What are *you* doing?"

Darn, he should have known *that* was coming. Oh, nothing, he thought, just getting some blood.

"I'm just going down the coast," he answered. "I need to check in with my Mom and see if everything's good."

If his permanently pale skin could have turned red with embarrassment, it would have. Going home to see Mom on the weekend, he thought, wanting to choke himself. Can his life get more boring? What a way to impress a girl!

"Where do you live?" she asked, probing with large, innocent eyes.

Hmm, a personal question he realized. What should he answer?

"Ah, I live in Ventura," he said. "Off the 101."

He was referring to the 101 Freeway that ran north to south along the California coast. He *actually* lived in Camarillo, a little further south, but the information was close enough, he thought.

"Do you go to the beach much?"

She was watching him closely. Her seawater eyes were searching his face. Was she trying to prolong this little chat, he wondered? Thomas thought that her cheeks were a little flushed, or was it the makeup she was wearing?

"Yeah, I go to the beach a lot," he answered.

Usually at night, he said to himself. Where is this going, he thought?

"I really like Malibu," he added, and its endless prospects for hunting.

He paused, "Would you like to go out to dinner Saturday

night? I happen to know a good restaurant right on the beach."

Whoa! Where did *that* come from? Was that his most charming voice and was he smiling at her? Was he *crazy?!* He berated himself.

"That would be nice," Briana answered.

Thomas stood there a few seconds before he realized that she had agreed to go to dinner.

"Hand me your phone and I'll give you my cell number," she said.

He handed her his phone, saying nothing.

She easily found his contact list, entered the number and handed it back.

"Call me and I'll give you directions to the house."

He continued to stare at her with his phone in hand. Singh was ready for the next shot, and Alicia was flagging Briana.

"Well, I'd better go," she said, as she turned to leave. "Bye…"

She looked back at him over her shoulder with a look of satisfaction. Did she know he was in shock, or was she used to dumbfounding all the guys? Thomas wondered.

He turned to walk toward the parking lot where the crew set up his trailer. Still thinking of his exchange with Briana, he felt like a normal guy, but he wasn't. He felt like he was back in high school asking a girl to the prom.

Why did he do that? He asked himself. What if she realized that there was something odd about him, as if she hadn't already? He couldn't date her. He certainly couldn't have a relationship with her.

Vampire Education 101, Rule Number one: *Don't get involved with the living*.

He started making excuses for himself, thinking Briana looked so good today. It felt so normal to be near her and talk to her. The memory of her scent reminded him that he was thirsty for some blood. *That* in itself was a reality check. Making plans to take her to dinner when he wasn't going to eat anything…obviously, he hadn't thought this through. He walked slowly toward the trailer, head down, continuing to talk to himself and trying to figure out how he was going to pull this off. Yet, his lifeless heart was thrilled, and he was walking on air.

As he reached the group of trailers provided for some of the actors, he noticed that the door on his trailer was slightly ajar. He hadn't locked the door. What would anyone take, he thought, his fake fangs?

He stepped inside and threw his costume jacket onto the built-in couch. His eye was caught by a plastic glass sitting in the middle of the small, oval table in front of the couch. He was not so much seeing the glass, but what was *in* the glass. He saw a semi-thick, dark, red liquid filled almost to the top of the glass.

Terror cut through him like a knife. Did someone leave a glass full of blood on the table in his trailer? He stood staring at the glass trying to think of what to do. His gut told him to get rid of it.

Thomas grabbed the glass and carried it to the back of the trailer where the toilet was located and emptied the glass into the bowl. The water turned red and left a residue at the water line. Not only did the odor of the blood hit his nose, but it had an odd smell to it - a metallic smell. He flushed the toilet several times to remove all traces of the red liquid.

Some of the blood splashed onto the back of his hand, and it was starting to burn. He moved to the sink, quickly turning on the cold water. The blood washed down the drain. The top layer of skin on the back of his hand also washed down the drain, leaving a nickel-sized, grey patch, smooth and shiny.

While wrapping his hand in a tissue, he knew by the smell that the blood wasn't human. It was probably beef blood; but what was the extra substance that caused the burn to his hand?

Panic began to set in. *Someone had guessed his secret. Someone on this movie set knew what he was. Someone was trying to destroy him.*

Who could it be? The fear gripped him! He ran through the trailer and out the door in a blur. In a few seconds, he was on a busy street but continued to run at full breakneck speed. He had to get away from there!

Running, Thomas quickly found himself outside the city of Santa Maria on a rural highway. He ran along the road not really seeing what he was passing, his mind still in-flight mode.

Maybe someone was watching for his reaction to the blood stunt. Were they lying in wait to see what would happen? Did they see him leave and follow him?

In his flight, Thomas passed road signs with a poppy flower and a number one. The fields in June were green and tan with vegetation, but he was in a fright and the surroundings were a blur. He came to a place where the highway crossed another road, and he veered to the new road trying to throw off anyone that may have followed. Finally, he felt the need to stop. The sun was beating down on his back and neck and he did not have his sunglasses.

He was starting to feel weak. Giving in, he sat down in a shady spot under a roadside, pepper tree.

Thomas pulled his cell phone out of his pocket, going straight for his contact list. He punched in Maggie Finchlock's number and hit the call symbol on the phone.

The phone rang twice and was picked up by his agent.

"Thomas?" she questioned, looking at his name on the phone screen as she answered.

"I'm sorry Ms. Finchlock, but I am going to have to quit the movie," Thomas exclaimed into the phone. "I have to leave right away!"

The crisis alarms went off, but Maggie lived in crisis mode half the time, working with young actors.

"Don't hang up," she said urgently, trying to keep him on the phone. "Are you all right?"

Unlikely, she thought. "Are you at the hotel?"

"No," he said, as he looked around. "I left."

Thomas paused, "I'm not sure *where* I am."

"Can you pull into a gas station and find out where you are?" Maggie asked, with a calm voice.

"No. Ah, I'm not driving."

What? What did he mean he wasn't driving, the agent thought? Maggie took the time to regroup in order to keep her voice as calm as possible.

"Okay, look around and see if you can give me any idea of where you are in Santa Maria."

As she spoke, the agent pulled up a city map of Santa Maria on her desktop computer.

"I don't think that I'm *in* Santa Maria anymore," Thomas

said, looking around for road signs. "I was on a road with signs that had a poppy and a one, and I think that I passed a sign for a town called Lontoc."

"That's Route 1, Lompoc is the town," she said, as she started punching at her keyboard.

"You walked all the way to Lompoc from Santa Maria?" she asked, with a disbelieving voice.

He had to be kidding. That would take some time. Maggie wasn't sure of the mileage but knew that the towns weren't next to one another. Route 1 was the scenic route that twisted through the rural, farm country in the area.

"Wait, there's another sign here pointing down this road. It's for a mission," Thomas said, as he looked closer. "La Purísima Concepción Mission," he read. "I think this is Purísima Road."

From his elementary education, Thomas thought this had to be one of the twenty-one, historical missions established by Spanish missionaries that went from south to north along the El Camino Real, the old Spanish highway. These missions were painstakingly preserved, religious outposts that originally interacted with the indigenous peoples long before California became a state.

Working fiendishly, Maggie had the map of Lompoc on her computer screen. For heaven's sake, what the hell had happened, she thought? Had Singh gone nuts on the set?

"Thomas, I want you to walk to the mission, and stay there," she directed. "It's going to take me at least three hours to get to you from here."

She paused to give him a chance to take in what she had said.

"Will you do that for me?" she coaxed, in a motherly

tone. "I'll come get you. I think you need to tell me what's going on."

The young vampire looked down the road. Three hours, that would be around five o'clock. He felt weak and didn't feel like running anymore.

"Yeah, I'll meet you there," he said, in a defeated voice.

"I'm leaving right now. Stay there," she emphasized, as she shut down the computer.

Maggie grabbed her purse as she went out the door and headed for the car. The afternoon traffic on the freeway would be murderous, she groaned to herself, not to mention trying to get through Santa Barbara at rush hour.

She would be *lucky* if she got there in three hours.

* * *

Thomas spent an hour waiting under the shade tree. The roadway was deserted. He looked at the sign for the mission again and decided to walk toward it. There was a building that looked like it could be a church attached to another long, low building set back off the road.

Thomas walked up the dirt driveway and made for the church. There was no one around on this afternoon, but the doors of the Mission were open, and he took that as an invitation.

The building was obviously of an old construction with thick walls painted white. He walked up the nave of the old church and sat in a front, wooden pew facing the alter. The building was so quiet, and little of the afternoon sun made it into the sanctuary through the small windows. The air was musty and cooler than outside.

Thomas put his head in his hands and tried to calm

himself. He looked at the statue of Mary and wondered if there was a God for vampires. Could he say a prayer, and have it answered, or was he a lost soul for eternity? The burden of his existence weighed upon him and the loneliness that went with it.

He silently said a two-word prayer to any deity that would listen, *"Help me."*

* * *

Between the car's navigation system and all of the road signs, Maggie had no problem finding the mission. She spotted Thomas standing by a tree near the roadside, just outside the entrance to the mission. He looked all right physically. Tall and lean, it looked like he was still wearing his wardrobe clothes from the movie.

Deep in thought, he looked up and saw the car.

She pulled the black Mustang off the side of the road and waited for him to get in.

"Hi, Thomas," she said, as he got into the seat. "Put your seat belt on," she instructed, and drove the car back onto the road, bringing it up to speed.

"So, tell me what's going on," Maggie encouraged. What brought this on?"

"I just can't do this," he said softly, looking down at his hands in his lap.

Thomas had been racking is brain for excuses that he could give his agent for leaving the movie set. He tried to rehearse some type of explanation for her, but hadn't come up with anything that would justify him quitting the movie. How could he explain that he needed to quit, to get away? There is no easy way to say that you have a vampire hunter after you.

"You decided this today and ran away from the set without your car?" Maggie paused, "Something must have happened."

She waited for some response, but he remained silent.

"Do I need to start with the twenty questions? Is it Singh?" she asked. "He does sometimes have a problem with young actors. I'm not sure why they put him on this project with almost the entire cast under twenty- five."

"No, Singh is okay. Usually, when he gets mad about something it's because I've screwed up somehow and we need to do another take. I don't think that he really dislikes me."

"Are you having problems with Briana?" Maggie asked, going to the next logical issue, not entirely crossing the hot-headed director off the list.

"No, she's been really great. I mean, helpful."

Thomas tried to keep any added tone out of his voice that would give Maggie the clue that he looked forward to every minute with his co-star. Now he may never see Briana again, he thought. He sank further into the car seat and into his funk. He would have to stand her up Saturday night. He shook his head silently.

"Well, this is getting us nowhere," Maggie mumbled, half to herself, trying to follow the navigator's directions for getting back to the highway. "So, why don't you tell me why I'm here and why you think you need to quit a job that half the guys in L.A. would die for?"

"I think there's something happening on the set," - Thomas paused - "something that I can't figure out. I'm not sure what it is, but I think someone is after me."

Maggie gave him a sideways glance. He was on the level. He was scared. He didn't appear to be faking it. After all, he *had* walked miles to get away, and he *obviously* didn't bother to get his things or his car. That's just nuts.

"No, this is a vampire movie," she said. "You are the vampire with immortal powers. You can get *them*, remember. You can do it all. They're the ones who should be running out of town," she chuckled, proud of her little joke while trying to lighten the mood.

He smiled sheepishly, "I know that sounds dumb."

Maggie drove for a while, and the interior of the car was silent, except for the mechanical hum of the engine. Scenery was flashing by as she quickly got up to her usual eighty miles per hour. Following the road, the Pacific Ocean came up on the right. The water looked bluish-grey, and the overhead clouds reflected the lowering sun's race to the horizon.

Maggie was the first to break the silence.

"Thomas, I believe you that something must be happening to make you want to leave the job. Can you tell me some of what's been going on that makes you feel so threatened?"

Thomas thought for a minute, then said, "Well, there was an accident with the lighting the other day. Briana and I were getting ready for the take, standing on our marks, when an overhead lighting rig came crashing down. I fell on top of Briana and the light rod fell on my back.

"We weren't hurt, just really startled and glad that we were okay. There was a lot of commotion, but no one could figure out why it happened. They had already blocked the scene with the stand-ins. We just thought it was a freak accident. We didn't get the scene done that day and had to do it the next day."

Maggie took this all in. "What happened today?"

"Now that I think about it, I probably overreacted," Thomas said, as he decided to play it down.

"I came back to my trailer, alone, after finishing a scene with Brianna at the campus, and found the door partially open. It looked like someone had been there, going through my stuff. I found a note on the coffee table that contained a threat, like, 'I'm going to kill you'."

He looked down into his lap hoping that she would buy his revised version of what happened.

"I guess I just freaked out. It was a threat to me personally. I remembered the lighting accident, and another accident I had the first week, when a harness broke during a stunt I was doing. I fell from the top of a staircase."

"What did you do with the note you found today?"

"I flushed it down the toilet."

Maggie looked sideways at him, then back to the road.

"I know that I should've saved it. I just kind of panicked and ran out of the trailer."

With one eye on the road and one hand on the steering wheel, Maggie picked up her cell phone and scanned her contact list for the person she was seeking and hit the number.

"Yeah?" came a female voice out of the speaker on the phone.

"Hi, Alicia. It's Maggie Finchlock," she said, allowing time for recognition. "Thomas Johnson's agent," she clarified.

"Hi, Maggie," Alicia acknowledged, and waited for what was to come.

"I'm here in the car with Thomas. We're on our way down to Santa Barbara to do a photo shoot on the pier that I scheduled for this afternoon. I wanted to get some sunset shots, if possible. Thomas was concerned that he left the set without telling anyone and said that you hadn't wrapped for the day."

"Yeah, we're still going at it. We'll be here as long as we have some light," the assistant director sighed.

"I have to apologize for the lack of communication, as this whole thing was my fault. I thought he was finished at three o'clock today. Thomas should have checked with someone before he left."

"We wondered where he got off to, but were able to use the stand-in. I thought that maybe he went back to the hotel, thinking we were done. No problem…just explain to him that he can't leave the set until he's told he can go."

"Will do. He is a little new at this and doesn't know all the rules yet. Thanks, Alicia. I appreciate your giving us a break."

"Sure." The phone went dead.

Thomas realized that Maggie had covered for him and gave her an apologetic look.

"Thanks."

The traffic thickened as the road came into the heart of Santa Barbara, and the car slowed to a crawl. This car smelled new and was plush with a tan, leather interior, but didn't seem to fit the driver. Maybe Maggie was nostalgic for the Mustangs of her youth, Thomas thought.

Surprised when they exited the freeway, he soon saw

that they were going toward the Santa Barbara waterfront. Maggie pulled the car into a crowded, restaurant parking lot and stopped next to a wall with a vibrantly painted mural of a seaside scene.

"Are we really doing the photography thing?" Thomas asked, not understanding why she had stopped here.

"No, this is where I get out," she said, as she handed him the car keys. "All the paperwork for the car is in the glovebox. Be sure to call and get it covered on your car insurance tomorrow."

Thomas stared at her, still trying to take in what she was saying, holding the car keys in front of him.

"Hope you like the black," Maggie said, referring to the car color.

"I can't afford a car, yet," he said quietly, knowing that there was no way he could make the payments on a new car, let alone the monthly insurance bill.

"You already did afford it," she explained, smiling at him. "It's a little perk that I got you. That's what agents are for. I knew that Pauline really wanted you for this job, but they're only paying you a little over union scale and giving you an introduction on the credits for the movie. They would have to pay any of the other actors up for the role two or three times what they're paying you. I asked for the car as a signing bonus.

"The car is paid for and registered in your name. Your Mom helped me with that one," Maggie said, smiling. "She's a nice lady. She's been dying to tell you. I was going to bring it out to your house this weekend."

A soft 'Wow' was all Thomas could manage, looking at the car.

His car was a hand-me-down from his grandfather and had long since seen better days. His Mom's small compact was over ten years old. There was no money for new cars in *his* family. This was totally unexpected. He had hoped that he would be able to buy a better *used* car once he was through with the movie.

"So, we're good? You're going to be back on the set first thing Monday morning?" the agent asked.

"Yeah," he agreed. "I'm sorry for all of the trouble this afternoon."

"I'm going to talk to Pauline and see if we can get some extra security on the set to keep an eye open for any weird stuff going on."

"Thanks," he said, but Thomas knew that a two-bit security guard wasn't going to be able to help him.

He would need to be extra observant and watch out for himself. The threat was far beyond anything that Maggie could imagine. He would have to be his own protector.

Maggie started walking away toward the restaurant back door.

"Where are you going?" Thomas called to her.

"My husband's here, and we're going to have dinner. I love this restaurant. Good to have an excuse to meet him here."

She waved, opened the door, and was gone.

Thomas looked down at the car keys and got into the driver's seat.

8

Publicity

Saturday arrived and Thomas was driving toward Eagle Rock to pick up Briana. He was nervous and apprehensive, not unlike before some of the first dates he had while in high school. The fact was he hadn't *had* a date since high school.

Okay, he did have some recent history of liaisons with girls since becoming a vampire, but he hadn't been emotionally invested in those hit-and-run encounters, which were mainly for the purpose of getting fresh blood.

This date was different. He was drawn to Briana, admiring almost everything about her. He wanted to spend time with her and just talk to her about so many things. In preparation for the date, he made sure that his thirst for blood had been satiated the previous evening by a trip to a well-stocked lab at a surgery center.

His pocket was filled with the favorite, lemon, hard candies used to help depress his natural urges. He hoped that she wouldn't take too much notice of his long-sleeved shirt and long pants on this hot day in Los Angeles.

Earlier on the phone, he had thrown out the idea of a trip to the Santa Monica Pier for the date. Briana readily agreed, citing fond memories of childhood visits to the famous landmark. Thomas thought that they could stroll the wooden walkway, take in the sunset over the Pacific, and then he would take her for a nice dinner. He was a little worried about the eating situation since he would have to fake some reason for his not eating; but, thought he could get through it without drawing too much attention to the issue.

Arriving at his destination, Thomas punched in the code Briana had given him to open the large, obtrusive gate which hid the house for maximum privacy. As the gate retreated, he drove onto an expansive, semicircular drive that led to the large front doors. Thomas took in the traditional, two-story house. The duplex he lived in – including the carport – would easily fit in the well-manicured grounds at the front of this house. He pulled the car up to the front walk and went to the door. Hesitating for a moment, trying to compose himself, he rang the doorbell.

Momentarily, Briana herself swung the door open, inviting him into a large, primarily white foyer.

"I just need to get my purse and a jacket in case it's cool down there," she said.

Standing by the door, Thomas watched as she swiftly ascended the curved stairway leading to the second story. While waiting for her to return he saw Joey Madison walking toward him through the spacious living room. He remembered her from the casting studio, and had heard Briana frequently mention her aunt and manager with whom she lived.

"Hi Thomas, how are you doing?"

"Good," he replied.

"How's the movie going? Are you enjoying acting?"

"It's harder than I thought it would be. There are a lot more action scenes than I first realized."

"I've read the script and there *are* a lot of action scenes, but I think that's something the audience will like," she said.

Then changing the subject, "Briana's been looking forward to getting out. Looks like you'll have a nice evening for it."

"Yeah, it'll be good to get down by the ocean. It's been so hot today," Thomas replied, trying to make conversation.

"Well, have a good time," Joey offered, but she could see that she'd lost the young man's attention as Briana rushed down the stairs.

Thomas took in a breath.

Every time he saw Briana she looked better. She was clearly in casual mode today. She wore skimpy, jean shorts, a flowered, halter blouse that flowed in soft folds to her waist, and she carried a powder-blue, sports jacket. Her luminous hair was tightly restrained in a braid and covered with a trendy, sequined, baseball cap. Large framed sunglasses added to a look designed to diminish the ability to recognize her for her acting roles. Finishing the ensemble was a small, rectangular purse hanging by a thin strap from one shoulder that matched the silver, bejeweled sandals highlighting her thin ankles and blood red pedicure. She smiled at Thomas and wasted no time going out the open doorway.

"Bye, Aunt Joey," Briana said, with a glance backwards.

She saw his car as they walked out.

"Wow!" she exclaimed. "I didn't know you had a new car. I thought you drove a different one up to Santa Maria."

"I did," he said, opening the car door. "That was the car I've had since high school. I just got this one on Friday."

"Nice," Briana said in appreciation, as she ran her hand over the tan, leather seat.

Joey closed the door after watching the young couple drive away. She mulled over her feelings about Thomas. She couldn't put a finger on it, but there was something odd about him.

However, she had to admit that Briana and Thomas were

a striking pair - her fair and pink, and him dark and pale. He was well cast as a vampire and was certainly photogenic with those piercing blue eyes. Yet, she felt that there was a hint of unhealthiness about him.

One thing that she could not deny was their attraction for one another was strong and couldn't be hidden, even to the casual observer. It would play well on film if it could be captured. Still, her real concern was for Briana, always Briana. She had never seen her niece so enchanted over a young man.

* * *

DeRossi arrived at the Santa Monica Pier late in the long, summer afternoon. He was fiddling with his new, digital video camera, which he had brought along with his Canon that was hanging in its usual spot from a strap around his neck. It was Saturday, and as usual, he had more than one place to be this evening. There was the shoot here on the pier, and later a premier at the Pantages Theater in Hollywood. For the photographer, the more packed the schedule the more he liked it. Money was not as much of an issue for him, since he was well set, and could take the jobs he wanted to do, but he liked a challenge.

He could have been taken for one of the many tourists that paraded the pier in his Tommy Bahama shirt, tan slacks, Ferragamo loafers, camera and all. He actually was securing a spot with an unobstructed view for the video and pictures he was hoping to get. The end of the pier, near the coastal highway, housed several restaurants that featured various types of seafood at various price levels. A revamped structure, taken over by a chain of shrimp houses, was opening tonight in an invitation-only gala. Some of the popular, young Hollywood crowd had gotten invites and a sought-after rapper, not often seen in public, was supposed to show up.

DeRossi carefully chose his position, knowing fellow paparazzi would be coming, competing for clear shots. Now he would wait, leaning against a decorative wooden barrel, wishing he had brought a hat.

* * *

The air was cooler in Santa Monica, and the sun had begun its decent. Thomas valet-parked the car in the small lot near the pier. As usual, on a sunny Saturday, crowds were drawn to the beach and the popular wooden walkway that extended well beyond the surf. The pier was a long one, and its giant pilings reached into the deep, Pacific waters near the shore.

Briana smiled as Thomas took her hand, and their arms gently swung back and forth as they walked onto the pier.

At the entry, there was a small amusement park off to one side with a roller coaster and Ferris wheel. The wheel's lights were already on and projected flashing colors as it went around.

"Do you want to go on the Ferris wheel?" Thomas asked Briana, guiding her over to that side of the boardwalk.

"No," she answered. "I'm afraid of heights. I don't like those kinds of rides."

"Roller coasters, too?"

"I don't like those either, I'm afraid," she answered. "But I *do* like the merry-go-round," she said, pulling him toward the wooden building that housed the old- fashioned ride.

"Do you want to do that?" She nodded, smiling.

"Okay, let's get the tickets."

Thomas had to admit that this was a great merry-go-round with its colorful assortment of painted horses and animals. Children ran between them, on a race to choose a horse. Some of the horses went up and down as the circular platform spun and the music played. Briana laughed as Thomas went down as she went up on her black pony. When the ride was finished, they got off, bought more tickets and went back in line to wait for a second ride. Later, they came out of the building hand in hand, laughing as they walked toward the ocean end of the pier.

* * *

Maggie Finchlock placed her second call to Carol Berman. This time she called her cell phone number. She hated to bother Carol on a weekend, but she felt that she needed to let her know about Thomas Johnson, and the things that were happening on the set of the vampire movie. She would not tell her that Thomas ran off the set, but she was going to emphasize the possibility of a problem.

"Hello," Carol answered.

"Hi, Carol. This is Maggie Finchlock," she said.

"Hi, Maggie. What's up? No problems with Thomas, I hope."

"Yeah, I am calling you about Thomas," Maggie began. "I had a long talk with him yesterday, and it seems that there are some things going on in Santa Maria on the location site."

"Let me guess. Singh is making his life miserable?"

"No, I wish it were that simple. It seems that there have been some accidents on the set," Maggie began. "There was a problem with a stunt harness, and Thomas had a bad fall. He was okay, and it was chalked up as an accident. Then there was a lighting accident where a light bar came down on him and Briana. It was a miracle that they weren't seriously hurt.

"Then on Friday, Thomas said that someone left a note in his trailer threatening to kill him. He was a little unnerved when he spoke to me. He's scared and doesn't know what to do. I tried to reassure him, and he agreed to be on the set on Monday."

"Good Lord, Maggie, this sounds serious," said Carol, making sure she was understanding what the agent was saying. "Did he show you the note?"

"No, he flushed it down the toilet."

"Great," Carol responded, with sarcasm. "I think I need to tell Pauline Mellick about this. If we ignore it, and something happens, we'll all be sorry."

"Do you think Pauline knows about the accidents on set?" Maggie asked.

"I don't know. I would think that she probably doesn't as long as no one was seriously hurt."

"What do you think? Maybe they need some extra security on the set?" Maggie posed to the casting director.

"I think this is important enough to let Pauline know about it. Her and Adam can decide whether or not to hire some security for Thomas. Keep this under your hat, Maggie. I'll talk to Pauline before Monday."

"Thanks, Carol," Maggie said, with relief.

"I'll keep you posted. We don't want Thomas quitting the movie," said Carol, now worried herself.

* * *

DeRossi was people watching, whiling away the time waiting for the celebrities to arrive for the restaurant gala. He noticed a young couple emerging from the carrousel. The girl looked familiar. He brought his camera up and zoomed the lens for a closer look, automatically snapping the picture. Yes, he thought to himself. It was Briana Stillwood, only minimally disguised with a cap, sunglasses and her hair in a casual braid. Snapping a second and third picture, he zoomed the lens closer and realized that the guy she was with was none other than her co-star in the movie she was filming. It was that guy from the restaurant that had mysteriously gotten the lead role in the movie with Briana.

DeRossi continued to take pictures as they walked on, Johnson dropping the star's hand and throwing his arm over her shoulders. This was interesting, the photographer thought. Maybe the two were dating. These could be valuable shots in the near future he thought as the couple walked on, oblivious to the crowds and one careful observer.

* * *

Thomas and Briana ambled down the pier toward its end. Kids ran in and out of the pedestrian traffic milling along on both sides of the boardwalk. A couple of police officers in uniform shorts and riding bicycles, continued their slow patrol, mingling with the crowds. A man with a trained parrot was drawing a group of people wanting pictures with the bird. Briana stepped forward, letting the parrot perch on her shoulder, while Thomas took the pictures on his cell phone.

The sun was getting lower in the sky, and the light was getting dimmer as its golden rays danced off the puffy clouds on the horizon. Whiffs of a cool breeze announced the procession toward the night.

As they approached the far end of the pier, the crowds had dissipated and the sounds of the waves hitting the shore were muffled. Thomas and Briana walked back and forth, looking over the railing into the water on both sides of the pier. Here, the dedicated fishermen manned the railings with fishing rods. Fishing lines were cast into the sea beneath the pier. The fishermen talked and moved from one pole to another as they waited for a catch. Each little group had a bucket of water. Some displayed their catch of small fish on a line.

Briana and Thomas found a free space along the railing, leaning against it, watching the sky and water. Nothing needed to be said as they were just enjoyed the evening. Life was at a pleasant stall.

Across the pier, a man yelped as he pulled in a fish. His small daughter watched as he removed the hook and placed the fish in a bucket. Soon, he cast his freshly baited line back into the sea.

Briana watched as the girl climbed up on railing, looking down at the water. The child continued to climb, and Briana saw that her father was not watching. In a panic, she started to yell as the girl disappeared over the side of the railing.

Thomas saw the girl fall and ran to the opposite side of the pier. Before he got there, the girl's father heard her sharp, little scream and mounted the railing to jump into the sea himself.

Briana ran after Thomas who had reached the railing

and looked down in time to see the man enter the deep water feet first. Not thinking, he mounted the railing and jumped.

Briana was horrified and stood paralyzed looking over the side at the ocean below. The man came to the surface struggling to swim with the unmoving child. Thomas surfaced nearby and swam to the man who was barely managing to stay above the surface of the churning water.

People along the railing were screaming, and more ran from the other side of the pier to see what was happening. Briana broke from the crowd and ran toward a nearby small building that was a bait shop. She yelled at the man behind the counter to call 9-1-1, telling him that two men and a little girl were in the water.

Not waiting for the shopkeeper to make the call, she started running toward the beach end of the pier. On the way back, the police had stopped on their bikes to see why crowds were gathered on one side of the pier. Briana stopped running when she saw the officers. Breathless, she struggled to tell them what had happened. One officer got on his radio, and the other lit out on his bike for the end of the pier.

* * *

Bored and leaning on the side of the pier by the restaurant, DeRossi perked up as he saw Briana Stillwood run up to the two police officers on their bikes. Her distress was obvious. DeRossi wondered what had happened to the guy she was with as he watched the one police officer tear off toward the end of the pier. After a moment, Briana followed, again running. Turning toward the other side of the pier, he noticed people lining up along one side and looking into the water.

Something was up.

DeRossi looked out toward the surf, seeing nothing but the waves hitting the nearby pilings and shoreline. Down the beach, lifeguards were scrambling down the ladder from their elevated perch. Two of them jumped into their Jeep, and drove to the shoreline with lights flashing, coming toward the pier.

DeRossi took out the video camera and focused the lens on the surf. Soon, he thought that he saw a head bobbing beyond the breakers. He hit the zoom. He got it! It was Briana's co-star, holding a child in one arm just above the water.

Johnson was moving slowly toward the beach. A couple of surfers ran into the water, making their way out through oncoming waves. They reached Thomas, helping him with the man he was dragging behind by the shirt. DeRossi kept the camera going as Thomas came through the surf, finally standing, and walking onto the sand with the child in his arms.

The surfers struggled, trying to get the unconscious man through the surf and onto the beach as the lifeguards arrived.

DeRossi knew that he needed to get onto the beach to get more footage. He took off toward the end of the pier.

An arm reached out to him, and he stopped. It was Nick Walenski, host of one of the TV entertainment shows, also at the pier for the restaurant gala.

"Hey, DeRossi, what's going on?" Walenski yelled.

"I got a scoop. Briana Stillwood's co-star just pulled some kid out of the water. C'mon."

"I don't have my camera crew yet."

"I've got some footage. Come on," De Rossi called.

When the two men got to the sand, they slugged their way through it and the gathering crowd, moving toward the shoreline. Ambulance sirens could be heard in the near distance. DeRossi didn't waste time and started to film as he walked toward the action.

Lifeguards were working on the man lying in the sand, trying to get him breathing. Briana had reached Thomas at the water's edge. The child was choking on seawater. Briana slapped her on the back as Thomas held her upside down.

The girl came up screaming and crying. In this case, the crying was a welcome sound. Wrapping the child in her jacket, Briana took her from Thomas, holding her close to calm her. Soon there were just muffled sobs coming from the little one, as Briana talked softly into her ear. DeRossi got it all on video.

Paramedics arrived, and between them and the lifeguards they were able to get the girl's father breathing. They carried him on a stretcher up the sand to the waiting ambulance.

Next, they came and retrieved the child, taking her to the ambulance. At this point, Thomas was standing off to the side with Briana, clothes dripping from head to toe.

Nick and DeRossi approached the pair.

"Briana, can you tell us what happened here?" Nick asked, as DeRossi filmed.

"We were at the end of the pier when the little girl climbed the railing and fell into the water. I think the man who jumped in after her was her father. Then Thomas jumped in. I couldn't believe it. It happened so fast."

"Looks like you're the hero of the day," Nick said, turning to Thomas. "What's your name?"

"Thomas Johnson," Thomas answered, running his hand through his dripping hair.

"And how did you happen to be here with Briana?"

Briana jumped in before Thomas could answer, "We're on a weekend break from the movie we're filming in Santa Maria. Thomas is my co-star on the film. We just took a drive down to the beach to see the Santa Monica Pier."

"What's the film about Briana?"

"It's a vampire thriller, and Thomas is the lost vampire."

"Do you mind if we show some of the footage DeRossi got, and mention the movie on our show tomorrow night?" Nick asked.

"I don't think the studio would mind," replied Briana, with a charming smile for Nick.

DeRossi stopped filming, thanking Briana and taking a long look at the wet, young man, pale as a ghost in the dimming light.

"You better go and get dried off, kid," DeRossi said, looking at Thomas.

Thomas stared after the man with the cameras, as the two men walked off together deep in conversation. The guy gave him the creeps for some reason. That was the *second time* he popped up out of nowhere. Was he stalking Briana? Thomas wondered.

* * *

Sunday evening, Thomas sat on the sofa in his living room with Pismo stretched out between him and his mother.

"Do you really think that they will put it on TV?" she said, with excitement.

"The guy from the entertainment news show asked if they could use the footage, and said that they would mention the movie," Thomas answered.

"Here's the show," she said, as the show came on.

Nick Walenski opened the show by reporting on Briana and Thomas and the rescue by the pier. They praised Thomas, giving him credit for dragging the child and her father to shore and probably saving their lives. They showed the footage of Thomas coming onto the beach holding the girl, and the footage of Briana and Thomas after the rescue. The TV host had spoken to the Checkmate Studio publicity department, and reported further details on the vampire movie, the young actor starring with Briana, and the probable release date for the movie.

"You're a hero, honey," Lynette Johnson said, with pride for her son.

"I just happened to be there, Mom. I'm glad to hear that they both will be all right."

His date with Briana had certainly not gone as planned. After leaving Santa Monica, he took her home and then drove home himself. She called him later that night to see how he was doing. She said she would see him on the set on Monday.

Monday, he thought. He was driving to Santa Maria tonight, after he made a blood run. He wanted to get some extra to take with him to stash in the little, blue cooler at the back of his closet. Getting blood up there had been a little difficult. He found a hospital just north of Santa Barbara from which he was lucky enough to get in and out with blood. He also found a dialysis unit that he was able to rob. One night, he drove all way down the coast to try a surgical center he knew about. His diet was a constant worry.

Then there was what happened on Friday. He had to start checking people out. Obviously, someone was aware of his secret. How would they know unless they shared his status, also being a vampire? Why they were after him he couldn't figure out.

Was he infringing on someone's territory? He didn't know. He just knew that he needed to be alert at all times and ready to run if necessary.

* * *

Pauline Mellick had just gotten off the phone with Adam Siegal. She had filled him in about the problems on the vampire movie set. It was Tuesday, and it had taken her an extra day to verify the reports of accidents on the set after Carol called her on Sunday. She spoke with Singh, who verified the lighting accident. The lighting techs couldn't explain the cause of the accident. Singh didn't know about the accident with the harness, but got Alicia on speaker phone, who verified that there had been an accident with a stunt harness. She also verified that Thomas had hit the ground hard and was knocked out. Dogman Booker said that it should never have happened.

Again, the accident couldn't be explained. Alicia said that Thomas refused medical care and disappeared before the paramedics showed up. He had reported to the set on time the following day as if nothing happened. She made him sign a release for refusing to be seen by a physician, prior to starting back to work. Pauline hadn't said anything about the threatening note to the movie's directors, but *did* tell Adam about it.

Adam green-lighted extra security for the set. She spent the morning on the phone looking for a tip on an undercover private detective for the vampire set. She was surprised at some of the information she found, using an ear-to-the-ground, LAPD detective friend. She got the number and made the call.

"DeRossi," the groggy male voice answered.

"Mr. DeRossi, this is Pauline Mellick. I'm one of the producers at Checkmate Studios."

DeRossi sat up in bed in his darkened bedroom, glancing at the digital clock radio reading one o'clock.

What the hell, he thought? How did Pauline Mellick get his cell phone number?

"Yes, Ms. Mellick. Of course, I know who you are. What can I do for you?" he asked, politely.

"I understand that a thank you is in order for the publicity you assisted with on the new Briana Stillwood movie."

"I was just at the right place at the right time. I was happy to provide the footage."

DeRossi didn't mention that he'd been paid well for the video he'd shot at the pier.

"You have a reputation of being very well connected in this town. Do you mind if I ask if you're still working as a private detective?" Pauline asked.

Another surprise for DeRossi.

Few people in the entertainment business knew that he had spent many years working as a private detective, prior to coming into some money and giving up the job for a camera.

"You have excellent sources, Ms. Mellick," DeRossi responded, quietly.

"Yes, a friend at the LAPD speaks highly of you."

"I turned my back on that profession several years ago. Why are you asking?"

"Can I trust your discretion, Mr. DeRossi?"

"Certainly. Not all paparazzi are immoral."

"We are having some problems on the set up in Santa Maria. There have been some accidents, and of late, there was a threat against one of our actors."

"Briana Stillwood?"

"No, actually, it's Briana's co-star, Thomas Johnson."

"I'm not sure how I can help you with that."

"I was thinking that we might come to an arrangement, Mr. DeRossi. We could place you on the set, saying that you are working for the studio, providing material for how the movie was made. You know, candid photos and behind the scenes footage on the set. You could do interviews with the cast and crew while trying to find out if these accidents were deliberate, and maybe prevent any more problems. You could keep an eye on Thomas and help protect him if he really *is* being threatened by someone." Pauline paused, giving the man a chance to think over the proposition.

"You would be paid as a private detective and all of your expenses would be covered. We would put you up in the same hotel as Thomas."

"Sounds like you have this all worked out," DeRossi said.

"We need someone that can move about freely on the set but has the clout of the studio behind him. Not to mention someone with your particular experience."

"It would be a change of pace," DeRossi said, pondering the job. "All right, Ms. Mellick. Will anyone but you know the real reason for my being there?"

"Only Adam Siegal. I'll call Singh and tell him that you're coming, and that you are to have full access to the set. The hotel is The Old Meridian on Main Street. Let me know when you get there. You can call me at any time at this number if anyone gives you a problem."

"Okay. Let me wrap up a few things. I'll head up there in the morning."

"Thanks, Mr. DeRossi."

He sat on the side of the bed, reviewing the information about the problems on the movie set. His instincts told him this young actor would be trouble, and he hadn't been wrong.

9

Pizza, Beer, and a Starlet

Briana sat in the middle of the king-sized bed in her hotel room. Propped up on mounds of pillows, she could not get into the TV movie she selected. Thomas was at the forefront of her mind. Once again, she was trying to figure him out.

Their enjoyment of last weekend's date initially went well. Briana was sure that Thomas was liking their time together as much as she was. The accident of the child falling into the ocean interrupted and prematurely ended the evening.

After leaving the pier, Thomas did not look well on the drive home. His face seemed paler than usual, and his lips were almost white. When Briana accidently touched his arm, she felt his cold skin – not cool – but still cold from his ocean swim. She understood the need for him to get home and get out of his wet clothes.

Even the atmosphere in the car held a chill in the air.

When they arrived at Briana's door they parted politely, small talk taking precedence. There was no hug. There was no goodnight kiss. Briana was glad that the little girl and her father were going to be all right, but she couldn't help feeling some selfish disappointment. As she climbed the stairs to her bedroom, she had to admit that the date hadn't met her prior expectations. She had so looked forward to a romantic escapade with her mysterious co-star.

She got off the bed, walked to the window and moved the heavy drapery back for a clear view. Her room, though large and comfortable, overlooked the hotel parking lot. She scanned the parked cars and noticed that the shiny, black Mustang was nowhere in sight. Thomas was gone.

Where did he go all the time? She wondered. His car was gone last night, too.

In fact, Briana had barely seen Thomas since Saturday. When she got to the makeup trailer on Monday, she heard that all of the vampires had reported early to the set at the bank building. Singh, Alicia, and Dogman reviewed the prior footage from the fight scene. They decided that they needed more close-ups of each vampire and retakes on some of the action. The lease on the bank building was ending, leaving only Monday and Tuesday to use the space.

Tomorrow he would not be able to escape her, she thought. Tomorrow they were to be filming one of the more intimate scenes between their characters, Lisa and Penn. She would have liked to have spent more time with Thomas before beginning the one-on-one scenes that would be emotionally demanding for both of them. With one last canvas of the parking lot below, she sighed and turned away from the window. She would go to bed with anticipation and a little anxiety for what the next day would bring.

* * *

It was Wednesday morning, and Singh got up before the sun. He spent early mornings alone with a well-brewed cup of black tea and meditations. He knew today would be a challenge on the set. He calmed his inner core, requesting patience from his gods.

After a phone call from Pauline Mellick at the end of the shooting yesterday evening, he sent a text to the other directors, production managers, and crew supervisors for all cast and crew to be on the new location site by nine o'clock Wednesday for a general meeting. He had gotten several responses requesting permission to miss the meeting for various reasons, so he sent a second text affirming that the meeting was mandatory for all. He was assured of cooperation, if for no other reason than curiosity.

The next location site was a semi-rural property of about five acres not far from the downtown hotels. It held a long, one-story, ranch house at the front, a large backyard with a horse corral, and at the far end an old barn. Singh first approved the location site last week and started filming there with Briana and the horse over the past two days. The rest of the production crew were due to be on site today.

The barn, where the fair Lisa brings the injured vampire Penn to recuperate, is the site of several scenes between the two characters. The paved frontage road that goes behind the barn, was to be used for another set of scenes. All of this, seeming to be out in the sticks somewhere, was actually only fifty yards from a shopping complex where the small RV city of production trailers could be set up.

Today would be the first filming inside the barn with Thomas and Briana. The set decorators were still working on the interior yesterday. A back corner of the barn was used to construct a fake tac room for horse gear, and also held a desk and a narrow bunk.

The clever thing about the set was that one wall of the room was easily removed, making way for cameras and lighting equipment for filming. Singh could have built a set in one of the sound stages on the studio lot, but he wanted the rustic look of the old barn's interior and the view of the landscape looking out from the inside of the barn. Besides, they had already filmed all of the scenes with Briana, and the actors playing her parents, on sets at the studio. Singh always went for the authentic when he could get it.

Finishing his tea, he put on his shoes and wrapped his long hair in his signature, bright yellow turban.

* * *

When Thomas got to the new location, he immediately went to the makeup trailer, which had become his usual morning starting point. He found a locked door and noticed the lack of production people that were normally milling about. He saw people standing around an old barn down a nearby, narrow road, and started toward them. When he reached the barn, he found the collection of cast and crew forming a crowd in an open space between a horse corral and the front of the barn. He craned his neck to see Singh climbing onto a low platform of boards that had been hastily constructed for the man of medium height.

Thomas's makeup artist, Colin White, came up to stand next to him.

"What's going on?" Thomas asked.

"Not sure, man. We were all told to be here this morning for a meeting with Singh," Colin replied.

Someone handed Singh a microphone, and after a couple tries to get it working, he gave a "Good morning", and a hush came over the loosely assembled group.

"Good morning," Singh repeated. "Thank you all for rearranging your schedules to be here this morning. I just have a couple announcements to make, then we can take advantage of the wonderful breakfast our catering crew has set up in the barn.

"First, I would like to introduce a new member to the production crew. Mr. DeRossi, can you join me up here on the platform?"

There was a pause as a man dressed in a purple shirt, with matching tie and black pants stepped up to join Singh, facing the group.

Thomas was astounded. Him again?!

Singh continued, "I would like to introduce Mr. Carlin DeRossi, who is here representing the Checkmate Studios Marketing Department. He is a distinguished photographer who is well known for his work in the American entertainment industry. Mr. DeRossi is here to collect behind-the-scenes videos and photography for the making of *Lost Vampire*. This material will be used as publicity and bonus material on the deluxe CD package for the movie. He will also be conducting interviews of cast and crew members. I know that you will all give him your full cooperation and answer any questions that he may have related to this production. Mr. DeRossi will be joining me today as a guest on set. I would ask you all to make him feel welcome."

A brief applause broke out as Singh paused.

Thomas could not believe that this guy was going to be part of the production team. He was just a freelance photographer, and now he was representing Checkmate Studios? How did *that* happen?

"My second announcement this morning has to do with our leading vampire, Thomas Johnson. Thomas, where are you? Come up here," Singh demanded.

Oh, no, Thomas thought.

Colin turned and started slapping him on the back.

"He's here," he said, pushing Thomas forward into the crowd, people stepping aside to make way for him.

Reluctantly, Thomas made his way to the makeshift stage to stand in front of Singh.

"No, come up here, so everyone can see you," Singh commanded.

Thomas climbed onto the small platform, squeezing in between Singh and De Rossi, wondering if this could get any worse.

"Thank you, Thomas," said Singh. "For those of you who may have missed the news last weekend, I would like to acknowledge Thomas here, for his acts of heroism. It seems that he and Briana were on the Santa Monica Pier last Saturday when a child fell into the ocean, followed by her father. Thomas, who is starting to believe that he *really does* have vampire abilities, jumped in the water and was somehow able to get the child and her father to shore. He managed to save two lives. Mr. DeRossi here, was able to film the event. Between him and Nick Walenski of *Life's Entertainment TV*, our movie - *Lost Vampire* - got some valuable publicity. So, a round of applause for Thomas - a true hero!"

A loud applause, complete with cheers, went on for what seemed like a long time to Thomas. All he could see was Briana, standing off to the side. She was leaning against a fence post, smiling at him.

* * *

"What's that guy doing here?" Thomas asked Briana. "Do you know who he is?"

"No, I've only seen him at Bluestones that night and last Saturday at the Pier."

"Now he's working for Checkmate Studios and is going to be on the set every day?" Thomas asked, with a voice of complaint.

"Yeah, he's a little creepy," said Briana. "I wonder how he talked the studio into getting such access to the set and the production crew. You heard Singh. The guy has permission to talk to anyone. He must know somebody high up in the studio."

Thomas and Briana were whispering as they remained on the barn's set between filming takes. In the scene that they were doing, Thomas was playing the wounded Penn, lying on the narrow bunk in the small tac room. Thomas had no dialog in the scene other than the occasional groan, pretending to come in and out of consciousness. Briana was sitting on a stool next to the bunk, where she played Lisa tending to the injured vampire.

They were on the sixth take of the scene. Technicians were trying to fix the overhead microphone boom, while light and camera angles were being fine-tuned. Soon the impatient Singh called for action and the filming commenced. There were at least fifty people in the old barn, but the only sound to be heard was the concerned Lisa speaking to the supine Penn.

DeRossi, with a camera hanging from a strap around his neck, perched himself high on the steps of a ladder leading to a loft area of the barn. He was across the barn from the filming, with an unobstructed, downward view. He snapped shots of the set and crew between filming episodes. His focus was on the participants, and the people on the periphery of the set. He needed to learn who was who, and who did what job. He wondered which one of these people, if any, could be a threat to Briana or Thomas - especially Thomas.

Pauline had filled him in on the three events, which required additional caution and security on the movie set. The first event, was the breaking of the stunt harness, resulting in a fall for Thomas; the second, was the lighting accident that could have been targeting either Briana or Thomas; and last, there was the death threat note for

Thomas.

Few people were aware of the death threat, and there was no actual evidence. DeRossi was looking for a connection between the events, one dealing with a stunt and one with lighting, which involved different crew members. The death threat could have come from anyone on the set.

The afternoon waned, but the filming of the moaning Penn and the worried Lisa continued. As the number of takes mounted, Singh's frustration became more apparent. The climate in the barn became warm and tense. Thomas could feel that Briana was getting nervous with her inability to please the director.

When Briana wasn't looking, Thomas slipped his fake fangs into his mouth. The director called for the next take to begin and quiet filled the barn. As Lisa leaned over the vampire, Thomas saw his opening. Suddenly he sat up, grabbing his co-star with a fang-filled snarl and diving his head into her neck as if to bite. Briana let out a surprised scream, then broke into laughter as Thomas put his arms around her. The crew, and even Singh, were laughing. The tension in the air dissipated and the director called a wrap for the day.

DeRossi watched the process for closing down the set for the night. Crew loaded equipment onto wagons and pulled them out the door toward the trailers. Briana was talking to a young woman as she removed her jacket and handed it over. Singh was in a conversation with a short-haired blonde, before abruptly leaving through the wide doorway. Thomas was talking to a thin, black guy. DeRossi quickly shot some pictures. Later, he would try to figure out the job positions of the people on set by what they were doing. He wanted to keep tabs on Thomas when filming was completed, but when he looked to where the young actor was standing a few moments before, he saw that the actor was gone. He scanned the barn. Man, Thomas had given him the slip.

Briana was also looking around for Thomas. Her elusive vampire had managed to make another getaway. She decided to have dinner and call him later.

Thomas was already in his car driving to the Pacific coast. He was going south. It wasn't easy being so close to Briana all day - not when he was thirsty. Just thinking about it, he popped a lemon candy into his mouth. He needed to get some blood.

* * *

The following evening Thomas was in his hotel room. He was restless, wanting to travel down the coast, but tonight he felt trapped. The previous night he managed to score some blood. He wanted to get some extra to bring back, but the surgical center was low on their stores.

He noticed that DeRossi was trailing him all day. The man had not approached him or asked for an interview. His tailing was not overly conspicuous, but the man seemed to be there with his camera every time Thomas looked around. They filmed at the barn again today, and DeRossi was on set. Thomas saw him speaking with the lighting director and to Dogman. When the lunch break was called, Thomas made a beeline for his trailer, where he remained until Colin knocked on the door and called him back to the set.

Thomas rushed to the hotel for a change of clothes, only to realize that DeRossi had followed him. This was probably not a good night to go out, he reasoned. He didn't want that squirrely photographer following him on a blood run.

After taking a shower to remove all of the makeup and hair gel, he put on some sweats and a t-shirt, settling in for a night of TV.

Early in the evening, Briana called. They talked about today's filming and what was on tap for the next day. The call ended on good terms, and both were happy with their newfound closeness when they said goodnight.

Briana was also spending the night in her room to hide out from Jennifer Weingart, who seemed to think that Briana was her dinner partner every day after filming. The girl was a gossip and always trolling for personal information that she could spread around. Briana was also aware that the girl had a crush on Thomas, always trying to glean details about him. Tonight, she would just have room service for dinner.

Later, Thomas was surfing through TV channels with the remote when he thought that he heard a knocking on the hallway door.

Immediately, the image of DeRossi came to mind. Or maybe it was Briana? He decided not to answer.

The knocking came again.

"Thomas are you there?" came a female voice.

It didn't sound like Briana, thought Thomas.

"Thomas," the voice came again. "Open up."

Thomas put down the remote and went to the door. When he pulled it open, he was surprised to see Jennifer Weingart standing in the doorway, balancing a large pizza box and six-pack of beer.

She sauntered into the room before Thomas could get a

word out. Her long, brown hair fell in thick waves around her shoulders. She walked to the small counter which held a coffee maker, put down the pizza box and opened it to reveal a large, pepperoni pizza. She set the beer down and removed two cans, which she popped open with a fizz.

"Dinner is served," she said, handing Thomas a can of beer.

Not waiting for a response from Thomas, she took a piece of pizza and made herself comfortable in the lounge chair near the window.

"What's all this?" Thomas asked, as his mind raced to deal with the situation.

"Well, I noticed your car in the parking lot, and knew that you didn't come down for dinner, so I thought I'd get a pizza. You like pizza, don't you?"

"Yeah, sure I like pizza, but I already had room service," Thomas said, sitting down on the end of the bed.

"I'm sure that you can eat at least one slice. Besides, pizza is good cold," she said, taking another bite and tipping the beer can.

Thomas took a sip of the beer while Jennifer continued to eat. When she finished the pizza, and guzzled the remaining beer, she went back to the small counter to discard the empty can and pop open another.

"What are you doing here?" he asked, deciding to take a stand.

"Briana stood me up for dinner," she said. "Besides, I've been wanting to get to know you ever since we got here, but you're never around. Where do you go all the time? Why don't you ever come down to the lounge with the rest of us?" she asked, continuing to drink the beer.

"I'm usually pretty worn out at the end of the day, and I don't feel like hanging out," answered Thomas, defensively. "I sometimes go down the coast in the evening to check on my mother in Ventura. She's been sick, and she's home alone. She's getting chemotherapy right now. It's just a bad time for me to be gone," Thomas lied.

"Oh, I'm so sorry. No wonder you go down there at night. Does anyone else know?"

"No, and please don't tell anyone. It's not something I want going around the set."

"Don't worry, Thomas. It'll be our secret," the girl said, with exaggeration.

The room grew quiet as Jennifer continued to drink the beer. Thomas took a rare sip from his can, trying to think of a polite way to get rid of her. She started watching the game show on TV, commenting on the contestants. During a commercial, she got up for her third beer… but who was counting?

Minutes dragged by for Thomas. He had to admit that Jennifer was beautiful, even with most of her makeup worn off. She had large brown eyes, a straight nose, and lovely, full lips. She wore a V-neck top that showed the swell of her breasts. His eyes moved to her neck where he could see a pulsation under the skin.

Jennifer saw him watching her and took it for a signal for her to make a move, so she did. She came out of the chair and walked to the end of the bed where Thomas was perched. Stumbling over his foot, she landed on the bed with a giggle. Then she sat up, facing Thomas.

Now that Jennifer was within reach, Thomas' senses began to betray him. Her wide eyes were searching his. Her breath and heartbeat quickened. The pleasing scent of her skin assaulted him. He could feel his teeth begin to descend. Where was a lemon drop when you needed one?

"Thomas…," she whispered, close to his ear, falling under his spell.

Defenses gone, he went for the vein and the warm rush of liquid filled his mouth. It had been over a month since he had fresh, warm blood. This was what he needed. The girl gasped with the shock of the bite, then struggled briefly, realizing the firmness of his grasp. The blood flowed and soon she went limp in his arms. Thomas continued to drink, until his thirst was satisfied.

Then, *reality* hit with a bang, and he withdrew from the unconscious girl lying on the bed.

He stood up at the end of the bed looking at Jennifer, swaying from side to side as the full effect of the alcohol started to affect him. He immediately berated himself. How could he have done this? Now what was he going to do?

He leaned over her and assured himself that she was still breathing. He took her wrist and felt for a pulse. He found the rapid, faint beat. He sighed with relief, then noticed he began to feel woozy. Jennifer finished three beers, but this was something more than alcohol. What else was in the starlet's system? Had she done some sort of drugs prior to showing up at his door?

Thomas sat down in the chair, continuing to reflect on the situation as his head got fuzzier. He tried to prioritize his thoughts. He had an unconscious actress in his hotel room. He had to get rid of her. He could take her back to her room, but he didn't know which room. Then deciding, with the beer, possible drugs, and the blood loss, he should probably take her to the hospital.

This was a mess, and he had created it!

* * *

Briana was in her room when a knock came at the door.

"Who is it," she called, into the locked door.

"It's Alicia," came the response.

Briana fiddled with the locks and opened the door to find the short-haired assistant director.

"I've brought you the rewrite on the scene for tomorrow morning. I tried giving Thomas his copy, but there was no answer at his door."

"Okay," said Briana, doing some quick thinking. "I'll see him in the makeup trailer in the morning. Do you want me to give it to him?"

"Yeah, at least he'll have a chance to look at it," she said, turning to leave toward the elevator.

Briana looked at the two copies of the script changes. Earlier, she was thinking about going to Thomas's room and knocking on the door. Sometimes she allowed her mind to wander about her and Thomas - alone - spending time together, waiting to see what would happen.

She looked down at the script change and saw a plausible excuse for knocking on the door of her co-star. Could she muster her courage? He was always polite to her. He might just take the script and that would be it, and she would say good night.

Or… he might invite her into his room.

Briana went to the mirror in the small dressing area outside of the bathroom. She quickly removed the oversized t-shirt and put on a lacy, pink camisole that went with her gray and rose, flannel, pajama bottoms. She ran a brush through her hair, swiped a pink lip gloss across her mouth, and slipped into her open-backed sandals.

She grabbed a copy of the script and slipped her room key into her pocket. She rushed out the door, quickly heading down the hall and turning the corner. Briana knew that Thomas was in room 2034, which he told her previously when they were comparing notes about the hotel and their rooms.

She abruptly came to a halt as she came around the corner. There was Thomas, coming out of his room with the body of what appeared to be a girl slung over his shoulder, her legs dangling down to his knees. Once the shock wore off, she ran up to him, as he staggered under the weight of his burden.

"What are you doing?" she asked, in a loud whisper.

Then, "Who *is* that?" she asked walking around him to see the top half of the girl.

Again shocked, "Jennifer? Are you kidding me…*Jennifer?!*"

"Briana, it's not what it looks like," Thomas said, in a low, desperate voice.

"Are you kidding me… *Jennifer?!*" she repeated. "What's wrong with her? Where are you taking her?"

"She's been drinking beer, and I think she's taken some drugs or something. She came to my room with beer and a pizza. She passed out on my bed," Thomas explained. "I'm taking her to the hospital."

"You *both* smell like beer," said Briana, perturbed. "Have you been drinking? You can't drive like that. What if you get stopped by the police?"

"I was just going to take her to the emergency room."

The elevator down the hall made a dinging sound, signaling that the elevator was at the floor. Thomas and Briana stood in alarmed silence waiting for the door to open. They both felt relief when it did open, and there was no one there.

"I gotta get her out of here!" exclaimed Thomas, thankful for the reprieve.

"Take her down the stairs," said Briana, taking charge of the situation. "I'll get my car keys and my purse. I'll meet you at the bottom of the stairs."

Normally, Thomas would have no problem getting an unconscious victim down the stairs, but he was feeling out of it himself and had to do one step at a time.

Finally, he reached the bottom, when he heard the door opening and closing above. He hoped that it was Briana, and it was.

"Stay here until I pull my car around to the door," she said, running past him to the parking lot.

Thomas cracked the door, and saw Briana pull the car as close as she could get to where the stairs exited. Thomas moved toward the car, opened the back-passenger door, and unloaded the still unconscious Jennifer into the back seat. He climbed into the passenger seat next to Briana, who began pulling out of the driveway before he could get his seat belt fastened.

Thomas punched the buttons on his phone, getting directions to the nearest emergency room in Santa Maria.

"It's down Main Street on the other side of the freeway," Thomas relayed.

Briana drove in silence following the hospital signs. She pulled over as an ambulance with lights and sirens was advancing behind her, and let it pass. Next, she drove back onto the road, following the ambulance that was leading to her destination.

The ambulance was parked at the emergency room door when Briana pulled into the parking lot of the hospital.

"Now what?" Briana asked, watching the activity as the ambulance crew got their patient into the hospital through the two, sliding, glass doors.

"Let me go check it out," said Thomas.

"You're not going to carry her in?"

"First, I have to see if the coast is clear. I don't want to be the one answering all kinds of questions… do you?"

"Okay, but hurry up."

Thomas left the car and walked to the ER patient entrance. Peeking through the doors, he saw that the waiting area was crowded even though it was after nine o'clock. There were too many people to bring the girl in.

He started walking back to the car when he noticed that the ambulance doors were standing open. He ran back to the car, pulled the beautiful Jennifer into his arms and ran to the ambulance. He gently laid her onto the vacant stretcher. Looking around, he sped back to the car and jumped in beside Briana.

Briana was taking in what she had just seen.

Thomas, effortlessly carrying Jennifer, putting her into the ambulance where she would be found, and coming back to the car at breakneck speed.

"Come on, let's get out of here," he said, as she stared at him in amazement.

Back at the hotel, Briana pulled into a parking space and

turned off the engine. They sat in silence for a few moments, both lost in their own thoughts about what they had done and what would happen the next day.

"I can't believe you and Jennifer," said Briana, shaking her head.

"There *is* no me and Jennifer. I told you, she came to my room and forced her way in. I didn't know how to get rid of her," Thomas tried to explain.

"She likes you. She told me as much."

"Look, I don't even *know* her, let alone like her," Thomas insisted.

"Really?" asked Briana, wanting more reassurance.

Thomas noticed a shadow appear by the car window beside him. Looking up, he saw that it was DeRossi. He let out a groan and got out of the car. Briana followed, coming around the car to stand next to Thomas.

"Where have you two been?" asked the short man, with long sideburns and a ruby earring.

"We went out for a hamburger," Thomas answered. "Why?"

"You went out for a hamburger in your pajamas?" DeRossi persisted.

Thomas looked down at his sweats.

"These aren't pajamas," he said defensively.

Then, looking over at Briana, he noticed that her attire *did* look like pajamas.

"Do you really want the public to see you looking like that?"

"We just went to a drive-thru restaurant," Briana piped

in. "No one saw us."

"Don't you both need to be on the set early tomorrow?" the man asked, changing his tactic.

Thomas started to get angry. A couple of guys from the crew were standing nearby at the fence for the outside lounge, drinks in their hands. Thomas could see that they were taking in the action.

"What's it to you, Mr. DeRossi?"

Thomas put his arm around Briana's shoulders and led her to the hotel doorway, blowing off the irritating photographer.

10

Love Scene

DeRossi reflected on the events of the previous evening as he watched Thomas and Briana with their heads together in conversation between takes. So far, it was a busy morning of filming in the antique barn. The floor was cramped, filled with too many people and too much equipment. They began rehearsal early. Currently they were preparing for the tenth take of the day, laboring through one after another.

Singh's patience was holding, telling the company that this was a difficult but important part of the film. He explained that they needed to persist until they got it right. What was right depended upon whom you asked.

In this scene, the young vampire Penn, has recovered from his near fatal injuries, thanks to the fair Lisa. The two characters are feeling a strong attraction to one another. They are in conversation, pacing around each other, with the open barn door in the background. Lisa, who is encouraging the strange guest, comes to stand in front of Penn, putting her arms around his waist. As Lisa looks longingly at Penn, he embraces her and leans closer. Then, almost by habit, his gaze moved to her exposed neck. Lisa watches his eyes change from blue to black.

For the first time, Lisa begins to see Penn for what he is – a vampire. Alarm and fear show on her face, and she steps back from his arms. Penn's hunger and desire for Lisa is apparent. He steps toward her, moving his head into position near her throat, only to break off at the last second. Realizing the possible ramifications of his thirst, Penn flees from her out the barn door. Lisa is left standing alone, with tears streaming down her face as she grapples with understanding the nature of her new love.

Not just the acting, but the technicalities of the filming are difficult for both actors. Using differently colored, tape cues on the barn floor, each actor has to be in the right spot at the right time. They have to recite their lines showing convincing emotion. They must move correctly for lighting and boom microphones to remain outside camera range. Always aware where the camera is, they can never look at it, only at each other. As the scene goes on, the camera moves in to capture a close up of the drama.

The tenth take went well. Singh was pleased, but he wanted one more shot for insurance. He called for a twenty-minute break. The crew scattered, many of them leaving the barn for the short reprieve. DeRossi remained, inconspicuously keeping his eyes on the two, young actors. Singh was speaking with the first cameraman when Alicia Perry approached and interrupted the conversation. She seemed upset. DeRossi leaned in, focusing on any interesting insights.

"…she didn't show up for hair and makeup. She needed to be on set for the scene with Briana this afternoon," Alicia said to Singh, somewhat agitated.

"Did you go to the hotel to find her?" Singh asked.

"Yeah, I went over to the hotel when I didn't get an answer on her phone. You won't believe this – she's at the hospital."

"What?" Singh exclaimed, with surprise.

"I went to her room at the hotel, but she didn't answer her door. Then, I went down to the front desk thinking someone could let me into the room to check on her. I thought that she might be sick or something," Alicia explained.

"Maybe she was partying last night," the cameraman interjected. "She's usually in the hotel lounge every evening."

"The hotel manager said that they just had a call from Jennifer's mother. It seems she showed up at the emergency room last night. When they got her stabilized, and she was coherent, they called her parents. They drove up here last night from Orange County and are with her at the hospital. Her father is going to pick up her things at the hotel and he'll drive her car home."

"What's wrong with her?" asked Singh.

"Not sure. No one knows. It can't be too serious if they're sending her home. Her mother is driving her. I'll have to call later," said Alicia.

"Briana might as well go home until Monday. We're going to be up near San Luis Obispo doing the chase scene tomorrow. I'm heading up there to check on the prep for that," Alicia reported.

"Okay, we're going to finish up here after another take. Tell Briana that she can leave when we wrap. She can have a long weekend," Singh instructed his assistant director.

DeRossi knew that the conversation between the two directors was about Jennifer Weingart, Adam Siegal's niece. He had studied the list of the cast and crew on the *Vampire Lost* production, along with the list of hotels with the room assignments. He was still matching faces to names on the set, mostly for the production crew, but he already knew Jennifer from covering Hollywood gossip blogs.

He was staying at the hotel with the actors, directors and camera crews. His room was on the first floor, and he knew that Jennifer, Thomas, and Briana were on the second. DeRossi had seen Thomas and Briana out together the previous night. He didn't know about Jennifer, but his intuition was telling him that Briana and Thomas had something to do with whatever happened to her.

DeRossi glanced across the barn to see Thomas and Briana walking through their paces for the next take. He knew that Singh would be keeping them busy for at least another hour. That was just enough time to go to the hotel and check out their rooms, and maybe Jennifer's. When no one was looking, he slipped out the barn door.

* * *

Briana was off to the side of the barn getting a touch up to her hair and makeup. Thomas sat alone on a bale of hay. He adjusted the long-sleeved, steel gray shirt that was open at the collar. The black, leather vest hung unbuttoned, highlighting the pendant with the dragon insignia hanging at the center of his chest.

He watched as the crew members moved around him. He saw the back of DeRossi as he rushed out the barn door and wondered what the man was up to. DeRossi had been on set all morning, but only took a few pictures with the ever-present camera hanging on a strap around his neck.

Briana thought that he was creepy, and Thomas had to agree, thinking the man had a sinister air about him. He was not big, but Thomas knew from their encounter at Bluestones that he was strong. He was also agile, seeming to pop up from nowhere at opportune times. DeRossi's heavy, dark eyebrows arched over black, deep-set eyes. His receding hairline was probably the reason the man kept the sideburns.

Then there was the ruby, teardrop earring. DeRossi was just odd, Thomas thought. The man's voice was unexpectedly low, soft and clear. The guy seemed to think he had the authority to confront Briana and him the night before. Thomas really couldn't understand why Singh was putting up with him hanging around the set.

Colin approached Thomas for last minute makeup.

"Hey, dude, did you hear about Jennifer?" Colin asked, excited to spread the latest gossip.

"No, what?" Thomas asked, with all innocence.

"She's in the hospital. She went to the ER last night."

"Really?" asked Thomas, signaling a need for more information.

"No one seems to know what's wrong with her, but it looks like she's going to be okay."

"That's too bad. I think she was supposed to have a scene with Briana this afternoon," Thomas said, making conversation.

"A couple of the guys are guessing it was probably a drug reaction."

"Does she do drugs?" Thomas asked, already knowing that there was more than beer in that girl's system last night.

"Not sure," said the black makeup artist, reviewing his work on the actor's face. "Bro, Singh is a nut about drugs. He'll throw anyone off the set if he finds out they're doing drugs. He threw two carpenters off the last film for using cocaine; but then, Jennifer has friends in high places. She'll probably get a pass."

Briana came up to Thomas, insistent on getting his attention.

"We're ready for the take," Briana said, grabbing his wrist with two hands, pretending to tug him off the bale of hay.

"Later, Colin," Thomas said, following his co-star, focusing on the task at hand.

* * *

When he got to the hotel, DeRossi went to Jennifer's room first, looking for more information. The door was standing wide open. The bed was still made, but all of Jennifer's personal effects had been removed. An empty hotel room, DeRossi thought to himself, entering the space.

The trash can by the coffee bar was overflowing, so he dumped out the contents onto the carpet. There were tissues, wrappers, used coffee filters and empty sweetener packets. He saw a Styrofoam food container and used, paper coffee cups. He squatted for a closer look at the debris spread out on the floor. His eyes settled on three, clear, plastic bags, only two square inches in shape.

Bingo.

Dime bags, each containing remnants of white powder. DeRossi confirmed that Jennifer was a user; yet, she was probably not a threat to the production of the film, or to Thomas. He would keep an open mind. Taking the incriminating plastic bags, he scooped the trash back into the can and left the room.

Next, he went to Briana's room. The maid's cart stood by the open door. DeRossi peeked into the room expecting to find the maid, but the room was empty. He heard the vacuum cleaner running in the next room, where the door also stood open. He slid into Briana's room, seeing the stripped bed with sheets piled on the floor. The closet area was cluttered, overflowing with clothing and several pairs of shoes. Makeup, a brush and items for hair were scattered along the bar below the mirror.

In the main part of the room, the desk held a phone charger, magazines and the hotel room service booklet.

Bedside tables held a couple books, an empty candy bar wrapper and a hairband. Scanning the room, nothing caught DeRossi as unusual. DeRossi heard the vacuum turn off and left the room, meeting the maid as she returned to her cart.

"Excuse me," he said, to get the busy woman's attention. "I'm working with the movie crew, and I was sent to get something we need from one of our actor's rooms. His name is Thomas Johnson, and he's in Room 2034. Would you be able to let me into that room?" DeRossi asked, in his most charming voice.

"We're not supposed to let anyone into the rooms, sir," the maid responded.

"Please. I'll lose so much time if I have to go down to the front desk. They're holding up the filming on the set until I get back with the prop."

The woman looked him in the eye and judged that he was being straight with her. There was an excitement in the hotel since the movie people arrived. The staff had been instructed to be helpful.

She smiled, "What was the room number?"

The gullible maid followed DeRossi around the corner and down the hallway, where he stopped in front of the correct room. He thanked her, expressing great appreciation as she used her pass card to open the door. The maid smiled back at him.

As he stepped inside, DeRossi saw that the maid service had not yet been to the room. The bed was unmade. The sweats and t-shirt that Thomas was wearing the night before were draped over the end of the bed. The desk and bedside tables were clear except for the room service menu and the TV remote.

DeRossi went to the closet and opened the door. A few pairs of jeans and long-sleeved shirts hung on hangers. There was a pair of Nikes on the floor. The duffle bag was empty. There was a small, blue cooler pushed back in the corner. DeRossi opened it only to find soft, blue, cooling packets.

Next, he opened a shabby backpack hanging on a hook. Inside, he found a clipboard with hospital forms, and a Los Arbores Hospital Laboratory Technician identification badge with Thomas' picture on it. DeRossi pulled out a wrinkled, white shirt…no…it was a lab coat. What was this? He pondered the possibilities for a few moments, then moved to the coffee bar.

The coffee maker was unused. There were no snacks lying around other than a full bag of lemon drops. The trashcan told its own tale. Sitting on top was a pizza box. After lifting the lid, DeRossi found the uneaten remains of the pizza still there. Removing the box, he found four empty beer cans, and surprisingly, two unopened cans. Other than napkins, there was nothing else. Had Briana and Thomas shared pizza and beer last night? He wondered.

He wandered into the bathroom where a small, toiletry kit sat on the sink counter. DeRossi unzipped it and peered inside: comb, brush, toothbrush and paste, sunscreen, and a small bottle of Polo cologne. There was no razor or electric shaver. Hmmm.

DeRossi had seen enough. The kid's belongings in the room were meager, but they pointed to a mysterious young man, raising more questions than answers. DeRossi left the room undisturbed, more convinced than ever that Thomas had his secrets…secrets that involved someone else, in some way that could provide a threat.

* * *

Thomas was walking around the new location site getting his bearings. The site was about a thirty-minute drive north from the hotel in Santa Maria. It was between the freeway and the Pacific coast. Alicia and Dogman were running today's filming, which focused on a chase scene involving the vampires. Thomas rode to the location with Kurt and Rory. DeRossi took up the front seat next to Dogman in the roomy Tahoe – there was no shaking the guy.

Prominent at one end of the location was a gray building made from cemented large stones. It was old and long, with a central peaked roof held up with great, wooden beams. The crew was packing up the giant, inflatable air bag that was used by the stuntmen the previous day for shots of vampires jumping off the roof of the building.

Today, the chase scene continued with the actors running away from the building, down the road and through a small forest of trees. The trees were not aged, but old and dense enough to produce the needed illusion. In the woods, a track was built to allow the camera to move along with the action. Using this set up, they would get film footage of the vampires coming, going, and close side shots of the chase through the trees.

The morning shoot was easy. Thomas would take off running down the asphalt road toward the trees, with Kurt and Rory in hot pursuit. Kurt and Rory liked and respected Thomas, both for his physical abilities and his down to earth attitude. Occasionally they would tease him, like this morning when they were driving through Pismo Beach.

"Don't they have a pier at Pismo Beach?" Kurt asked.

"Yeah, I think so," Rory played along.

"Maybe we should take Thomas out there and throw some poor schlep into the ocean. Then Thomas could jump in and rescue him…DeRossi, here, could film it."

"That's a great idea. Think of the publicity for the movie," Rory quipped.

Dogman and DeRossi chuckled from the front seat. Kurt reached over and slapped Thomas on the back. Ha, ha.

That afternoon the crew was preparing for the race through the trees. Each vampire would be running with Thomas leading the way. Once a few group shots were taken, each actor would be filmed separately. Alicia was calling the action and had a real vision of what they were trying to achieve as an end product. Dogman was on duty for whatever he was asked to do, always supporting his team of actors. DeRossi was prowling around the outskirts with his camera equipment for pictures and videos.

The afternoon went along with Alicia putting demands on the lighting crew as the light changed along the chase route among the trees. The group scenes showing Thomas and the other two vampires running through the trees were completed, as were the individual front and side views with Rory and Kurt. Last to be done were the shots of Thomas. He would run along the path as the camera ran on its track next to him, pacing him, to catch the fleeing vampire's profile. Alicia wanted several takes, even though they had all gone well. She knew Singh, and she wanted to give him plenty of film for editing. Alicia called for a fifteen-minute break, after which they would finish the last filming of the day, with Thomas running toward the camera through the trees.

After the break, Thomas stood on his mark at the edge of the trees. The camera had been placed at the other end of the track with the lens facing Thomas. The plan was for

Thomas to run toward the camera. The cameraman would be moving the camera along the track toward Thomas as he was running into the camera, producing an unrealistic speed to the shot.

When they were ready, Alicia called for action and Thomas started his run. The take was completed. Alicia decided to add more lighting, which took a few minutes to set up. Colin fixed Thomas' hair and added to the makeup. DeRossi took some pictures of Thomas and Colin using the long-angle lens on his camera.

Thomas was ready to go. The cameraman gave the signal that he was ready. Thomas saw DeRossi at the end of the track, his camera poised for a repetitive burst of pictures, attempting to capture the action.

Alicia called, "Action!"

Thomas started his run. By this time, he knew the path through the trees and amped his speed. The camera rig was moving toward him from the end of its track.

Suddenly, Thomas tripped and flew through the air to the ground. He hit hard with a thud. He heard branches breaking and felt the shock of a heavy load hit across his shoulder and head, as he sank into blackness.

DeRossi was the first to reach the fallen actor. He quickly moved toward Thomas' head, lifting the fallen tree from the unconscious actor. Dogman and the cameraman were next to get to Thomas, turning him over to assess the damage.

Unbelievably, he groaned with the first signs of consciousness. Alicia arrived and stood over the men on their knees around Thomas.

"Should I call for paramedics?" she asked.

Thomas groaned again as Dogman was checking out his arms and legs for any breaks. His eyes opened with a sharp moan when Dogman got to his right shoulder which had taken the brunt of the hit from the fallen tree.

"Hey, kid," Dogman said, while watching Thomas come into the picture.

Thomas tried to sit up, and Dogman helped him.

"We need to get him the hospital to get him checked out. I think he needs an x-ray or a CT scan, or something!" Alicia's voice was shrill.

"What happened?" asked Thomas, raising a hand to his forehead.

"You tripped and went flying. Then a tree came down on you, Dogman explained. "How do you feel?"

"I just need to sit here for a minute," Thomas said, quickly coming into reality.

Colin reached the scene, having run from the trailer up by the stone building. He handed Thomas a bottle of water in an effort to help. Thomas opened the bottle. Instead of taking a drink, he poured the cool liquid over his head, then shook it off like a dog after a bath.

"Well, there goes the makeup and hair," Colin said, sarcastically.

Thomas let out a small laugh, and the tension surrounding him was broken.

"Do you want to try to stand up?" Dogman asked.

"Yeah, I think I can get up," Thomas replied.

Dogman took charge. "C'mon, let's help him get up and walk him back to the truck."

Then, "Wrap it up, guys, we're done here!" he shouted to the small crowd of crewmen that had accumulated.

"Get him to the truck and take him to the nearest hospital. We have to get him checked out!" Alicia insisted.

Thomas got up with the help of Dogman and Colin, one on each side. By the time they reached the Tahoe, he was walking with little support. Colin got an ice pack from the makeup trailer and handed it to Thomas for the lump on the side of his head.

"Dude, you have one hard head," Colin remarked, as Thomas was sitting in the front seat of the SUV.

"Now you sound like my mother," Thomas said, now fully alert, trying to get the ice pack in the right spot.

Dogman piled into the driver's seat and started the engine.

"Colin, get in and come with us, just in case I need some help."

Once on the freeway, Thomas asked, with some trepidation, "Where are we going? Back to the hotel?"

"Alicia's right, kid. We need to have you checked out by a doctor. The studio is liable in case anything happens to you after the accident," Dogman answered.

"I feel okay. I'm just a little sore," Thomas said, realizing he was in danger of discovery.

"You may feel okay now, but what if you have a concussion? Head injuries are nothing to fool around with," Dogman said, with determination.

Twenty minutes later they pulled into the parking lot of the hospital, Dogman parking near the emergency room walk-in entrance. Dogman and Colin walked beside

Thomas into the building. Colin stayed with Thomas while Dogman went to the desk, getting the paperwork started. Thomas was noncommunicative in a quiet panic.

After twenty minutes, they called Thomas' name, and a nurse led them back to a small room.

"Look, we have a possible heart attack on the way in by paramedics. It might be a while before we can get to you," the nurse explained to Dogman and Thomas.

When she left the room, Dogman looked at Thomas, "How are you feeling?"

"I'm okay, really. Just a little sore."

"Since we'll probably be here for a while, do you mind if I run Colin back to the hotel? I'll come right back."

"Sure, I'll be good here." Relief filled Thomas as Dogman left.

Thomas was off the exam table in a flash. The only thing that he liked about emergency rooms was that they were a convenient place to assure the viability of his zoned-out victims.

He opened the door and peeked into the hallway. The coast was clear. Rather than going out the way he came in, he decided to go down the hall leading to the interior of the hospital. He made his way, walking slowly and directly.

Passing the nurse's station, currently unmanned due to the code blue that was recently announced over loudspeakers, he saw an unattended lab cart.

The gods were with him today, he thought, gazing at two units of red blood just sitting there. He did a quick look around and grabbed the blood, slipping them into his shirt and pulling his vampire vest closed. There were some strange looks as he passed through the lobby and out into the cooler air of the evening, but he had escaped. He would make his way back to the hotel, get his car, and head south in the Friday night traffic.

* * *

Back at the filming site the crew was packing up the equipment. DeRossi saw Dogman take off with Thomas. In all of the activity, he saw Alicia by the trailer, on the phone, probably reporting the accident to Singh.

DeRossi was looking around the wooded area near where Thomas fell. Prior to the accident, he had his camera set to automatic to take a succession of photos when Thomas started his run. Now, he moved the camera to the light and started going through the pictures capturing the young actor's fall, and the collapse of the tree. He wasn't sure what he was looking for, other than anything unusual. Going back to the start of the action, DeRossi paused on a picture a couple frames before the fall. He applied the zoom to the shot, confirming his fears, and started to scour the brush and carpet of leaves along the path.

He almost missed it. He found a bundle of coiled, clear, heavy Dacron fishing line. It was anchored to a small tree. Wherever it had been anchored on the other side of the path, it must have come loose when Thomas tripped, recoiling back to the tree. DeRossi used his pocketknife to cut the line away, gathering it into a ball and stuffing it into his pocket.

Next, DeRossi went to the tree that had come down on Thomas. It was not a large tree, the trunk being less than a foot in diameter. He followed the tree trunk back to its stump, which showed the lighter colored wood of a clean cut. He snapped a few pictures. Here was the evidence that Thomas had run into a trap. Somehow the tree had been rigged to fall when Thomas hit the trip wire.

DeRossi hailed one of the lighting crew and asked for a ride back to the hotel. He had a phone call to make.

* * *

Everyone was tense inside the old barn on Monday morning. This was the day that Briana was anticipating ever since she heard that Thomas had gotten the part in the movie…the love scene. He was still in the makeup trailer when she came onto the set. Script in hand, she reviewed her lines – again.

Singh was on the set unusually early to supervise the crews. Alicia Perry was conspicuously absent. Rumors were that she had been fired, but there was no confirmation. Even though most of the actors and crew had gone home for the weekend, the story of Friday's accident in the woods had spread like wildfire via phone and text. Kurt and Rory were relieved when they saw Thomas turn up early that morning.

Possibly the reason for the raised tension in the air had to do with the guests that were here for today's filming. The arrival of the chauffeured, black limo turned all heads and set the tone for the day. Pauline Mellick stepped out of the back of the limo in the parking lot full of studio trailers, but she hadn't come alone. Adam Siegal climbed out after her, wearing a suit and tie, and his authority as head of the studio.

Pauline went straight to Dogman Booker, spending some time in conversation with him. Next, she and Adam went to the makeup trailer to find Thomas, dismissing Kurt, Rory, and Colin before closing the door. Soon they came to the barn, standing in conversation with Singh. It was clear that Singh was not happy, but he was doing his best to maintain a professional hold on his set.

Briana was shocked to see the two producers.

Of all days for them to show up, why today? Thomas walked into the barn and came to stand next to Briana. He popped a lemon candy into his mouth, picking up on Briana's anxiety.

"Hi," he said. "What's wrong?"

"Are you serious? We're going to have to do this scene with the producer and studio head on set!" she whispered.

"Do you know your lines?" he asked, calmly.

"Yes, I know my lines!" she whispered back at him, heatedly.

Thomas put his arm around her shoulders, leaning his head down toward her ear so that only she could hear him, "Well then, we've got this, don't we?"

Thomas was right. Once they were both situated on the small cot in the pretend tac room, Briana's acting experience took over. The duo went through their lines faultlessly, only stopping before the kiss at the end of the scene.

The set became deathly still, everyone in fear of a misstep caused by their error. Singh sat in his raised chair after checking the view of the small, manufactured room from both cameras that would be filming. Pauline and Adam stood behind the director. In the hush, he called for action, the scene board clicked, and Briana started her lines.

Lisa spoke with emotion. Penn listened intently, with shadowed eyes fixed upon the subject of his desire. He raised a hand and stroked her hair, then the side of her face.

The longing on their faces was blatant. Lisa put her outstretched hands against the chest of her vampire.

As Thomas and Briana spoke, Singh was aware that the actors had gone off script.

They were adding dialog, prolonging the tension prior to the kiss. The cameras kept rolling.

Lisa could smell the sweet aroma of a lemon drop as Penn lowered his face toward her.

"I love you. I never want to leave you," Penn said, in a soft, clear voice.

He gathered Lisa in his arms and lowered his head to cover her lips with his.

The kiss was prolonged. Singh allowed the cameras to continue.

When the kiss was finished, Briana laid her head against Thomas' chest, content in the moment. His arms were still around her and her heart was pounding. She heard Singh call 'cut' to end the scene.

Thomas did not let go of her immediately, so she stayed, allowing her emotions to ebb in the silence. Then she realized that there *was* silence. Her ear was against Thomas's chest, but she heard no heartbeat.

11

Night Shoot with Pyrotechnics

Adam Siegal and Pauline left Singh to get on with things after watching Briana and Thomas film the love scene. Now, DeRossi sat in a booth at what was probably the only New York style delicatessen in Santa Maria. Across from him, he watched as Adam Siegal piled lox onto his bagel. Pauline Mellick sat next to him, starting in on her vegetable omelet. DeRossi was not there to eat. He was there to report his investigative findings to Pauline regarding the accident during the stunt on the previous Friday.

Today, the two producers deliberately showed up on set to make a point – to Singh and to anyone else that was trying to put the production in jeopardy.

Last week, Siegal had gotten an earful from his sister after she arrived home with Jennifer, just discharged from the hospital. His sister was furious, even though Jennifer admitted to using drugs the evening of her hospital visit.

The wayward starlet still couldn't remember how she got to the emergency room – the whole evening was a blur, or so she said. The doctor diagnosed her with anemia, probably due to poor eating habits. His theory was that Jennifer had gotten some tainted drugs and had a rather severe reaction. Adam assured his sister that he would look into it.

"Do you know anything about what happened to my niece? She ended up in the hospital and no one seems to know how she got there," Adam asked.

DeRossi knew that he needed to tread lightly with Siegal. He didn't want to tell the man that he thought Thomas and Briana had something to do with the happenings of the evening in question. He had only a suspicion, and no evidence.

"I'd just gotten here when all of that happened. I've heard that Jennifer was spending her evenings down in the hotel lounge hanging out with the crew. There was some drinking going on, but everyone I've talked to denies seeing anyone use drugs. Singh seems to be a stickler on drugs and will throw anyone off the movie that is caught using. I don't think what happened to Jennifer had anything to do with the other accidents that happened on the set," DeRossi said.

"We spoke with Dogman Booker this morning. He answered all of our questions and is still under the impression that what happened to Thomas on Friday was an accident," Pauline informed DeRossi. "He was upset with Thomas for skipping out on being seen by a doctor after the accident."

"Oh, there is no doubt that what happened on Friday was *not* an accident," DeRossi emphasized. "Right after they took Thomas off the set, I did some digging around. Here is the fishing cord that was used to rig a trip wire."

DeRossi pulled out a clump of coiled, thick line from his pocket and put it on the table.

"Would this be strong enough to cause a fall?" Pauline asked, examining the line.

"Thomas was running down a path toward the camera. I was at the end of the path taking my own shots. They were using the same pathway all afternoon, so everyone knew the course. The tracks for the camera rig ran along one side of the path. Thomas was told to run at full speed with the camera moving along the track toward him. He had already done a practice run.

"I found this line later, secured to a tree. It must have been strung across the path at ankle height. When Thomas hit it, he went flying forward. I'm not sure how the tree was rigged to come down, but I *did* find where it had been sawed at the trunk.

"Here are the pictures I took of Thomas prior to hitting the wire…during the fall…and here you can see the tree coming down. This is a picture of the freshly cut tree trunk that I took later."

DeRossi spread the pictures out in a line on the table.

"Oh, my God, I didn't realize the tree was that big! This could have killed him!" Pauline exclaimed.

"Well, it did knock him out. Me, Booker and the cameraman were the first ones to get to him. We moved the tree off, and Booker checked him for any broken bones. Thomas regained consciousness pretty quickly."

"Who was in the vicinity right before the call for action?" Siegal asked, realizing that there was a problem with a deliberate attempt to harm Thomas.

"Alicia called for extra lighting just before the shot, because the afternoon light was changing, so there were the lighting people. The camera crew was there. I don't know, there were a lot of people milling around while they were getting ready for the filming."

"I just don't get it," said Pauline. "We've had several accidents, all seeming to target Thomas...but why? Nobody even knows who he *is*. Why wouldn't they be targeting Briana? If someone wanted to hurt the production, *that* would make more sense."

"This may not have anything to do with the movie," DeRossi hypothesized. "This may have something to do with Thomas. I'm going to look into his background to see if I can learn anything. Everyone I've talked to will tell you that he has a way of staying to himself when he's not on set; yet, everyone seems to have good things to say about him."

"It has to have something to do with the movie. A stranger wouldn't be able to get onto the set and stage these accidents," said Adam. "What about Booker?"

"No. I've talked to him," said DeRossi. "That guy is very responsible and thinks of the actors and stunt men as his combat team. Nobody's more upset about these accidents than he is. He's so straight he squeaks when he walks."

"Well, Alicia's off the production. I called Singh after I talked to her on Friday," said Pauline. "Singh was delegating too much to her. I brought in Roger Cooper to replace her for the rest of the filming but made it clear to Singh that I expect him to be on the set for *all* filming. We only have two or three more weeks on location here, and they start the night filming next week."

"Do you still want me to stay?" DeRossi asked.

"Yes," said Pauline. "We wouldn't know what happened last week if you hadn't been there to look around. You've confirmed that someone is threatening Thomas. Interview more of the cast and crew. See if you can dig up anything. Stay close to Thomas and Briana."

"*Those two* seem to be getting along well enough," Siegal said, referring to the morning's filming of the love scene. "The kids should love it, *if* we can get this film finished."

DeRossi was lost in thought. He decided to follow his intuition and learn whatever he could about the strange, young actor. He knew that Thomas was hiding something and planned to find out what that was. He knew it could be the key to what was going on.

* * *

"Hey, Johnson!" Dogman Booker called to Thomas.

Thomas was on his way back to his trailer. He stopped to allow the stunt director to catch up with him. The man didn't look happy, and rarely called him by his surname.

"I have a bone to pick with you. What's the idea of letting me sit in the ER waiting for you on Friday? What the hell happened?"

"They left me in that room for two hours and never came back. I felt okay, so I finally just left. I didn't see you," Thomas tried to explain.

"I told you that I was coming back after I took Colin back to the hotel. I sat there for almost three hours before I went to the desk to ask about you. They came back and told me that you had left without being seen by the doctor."

"Well, how long was I supposed to wait?" Thomas asked, defensively.

"Look, kid, this is how it works. If you get so much as a scratch during a stunt you need to get medical clearance before you can come back on the set. Twice now you've skipped out on being checked by a doctor after a bad fall. If Pauline Mellick hadn't bailed you out this morning, you wouldn't be here. These are union rules and you're putting the studio at risk."

"Look, I'm sorry. I really didn't see you waiting for me," Thomas said, contritely.

"Okay, but don't let it happen again."

Then in a more casual tone, "We're going to be working nights starting next week and there are lots of action scenes.

I'm going to be on you like dandruff to make sure that there are no more mishaps. You're just damn lucky that you have a head like a brick."

"Yeah, I know," said Thomas.

However, his thoughts were elsewhere. He was sure that he was being pursued by someone since these so-called accidents were obviously orchestrated. He racked his mind for a clue of who would be after him. Someone knew by now that he didn't go down easily. There was also the glass of blood in his trailer. Someone knew his secret…but who?

If he weren't immortal, he would probably be dead by now. A shiver of fear went through him. He would have to be more vigilant since he couldn't possibly guess what his pursuer would try next.

* * *

It was a bright, sunny morning. Briana knew this because she had seen the sun come up. Now, she was trying to go to sleep after being up all night. The whole crew was trying to get used to the change in hours since the night filming started. She reported to hair and makeup by seven, filming began at nine - after sunset, and they worked until four or five in the morning when the sky began to get light. The daytime hours are long at this time of year, with the sun rising early and setting late.

Only Thomas was doing well with the change of hours. He claimed that he was a night owl. He was wide awake while she was dragging herself around all week.

Her body was not adjusting. Thomas told her that all the coffee she was drinking made her 'grouchy'.

No, she was just going around feeling like a zombie. These were the nights of the walking dead.

The more she pressured herself to get to sleep, the more she couldn't, even though she felt tired. She got out of bed and secured the heavy drapery so that the daylight was not filtering in through the center opening. She turned the portable fan sitting on the nightstand to the highest setting, hoping that its ongoing hum would block out any daytime noise. She crawled back into the large bed, rearranging the pillows and bedsheets for maximum comfort, and sighed.

As she settled in, thoughts of Thomas filled her mind. They had become very close during the filming. Briana knew that his feelings for her were strong. He was demonstrative on the set, holding her hand or casually draping his arm over her shoulders. In private, he held her close, and his kisses were passionate. When he looked into her eyes she was under his spell. She loved being with him.

It was only when she was alone that doubts about him and their relationship began to creep in. Thomas had many little quirks that made him odd.

There was the thing about food.

In all of the time Briana had spent with Thomas, she had never seen him eat so much as a hamburger. He would be on the set when all of the catered food was laid out. Everyone would be eating, but not Thomas.

Frequently he would just disappear on meal breaks. He had a habit of walking around the set with a half empty water bottle, or a can of cola, but she couldn't remember seeing him drink it.

Other than their first date, he never asked her out to eat. When they did go out, food was not on the menu. On the occasions when she went to his hotel room, the place was empty of any food except for the lemon drops - always the lemon drops. They don't count as food, do they?

When she asked him about it, he confessed to her that he was anorexic with a phobia of eating in front of people. He went into a story about a doctor, an eating disorder specialist who he was seeing for the past few years. Then he talked about how his mother was always trying to get him to eat, which seemed to make his condition worse. He said that the more he thought about the need to eat, the more he didn't want to eat, and so on…

There was also the issue of secrecy.

Thomas was very secretive about his personal life. It wasn't that he lied to her, because she had never caught him in a lie. He just didn't tell her anything.

Oh yes, he spoke of his mother and dog and his life growing up. Thomas talked about high school and being on the football team. He sometimes spoke of working at the restaurant in Malibu. He said how he loved to go out on the beach at night.

Otherwise, when it came to his privacy, he was guarded.

One thing Thomas never spoke about was the future. There didn't seem to be any long-range plans for his life, or even thoughts about what he would do when the movie was done. He seemed to live day by day, as if it could all suddenly end. She sensed an underlying fear in him. Also, he never spoke of their *future*. Briana always felt that she was on the edge of a cliff, and he was looking back over his shoulder. She didn't know if there *would be* a future for them.

The fan hummed in the background as she drifted off to sleep to thoughts of Thomas, thoughts that included doubts that hung in her mind like cobwebs.

* * *

Singh was in his element with the night filming. The director was well known for night scenes. He and his lighting director meticulously planned the lighting. An annoyance of Singh's were movie scenes that were so dark, or so poorly lit, that the viewer couldn't see the action, or the details of the actor's expressions. Singh knew how to backlight a scene. He knew every subtle light and filter to give him the right effect. Tonight, they would film the character of Lisa finding the handsome, wounded vampire.

"What *is* that by the side of the road?" Lisa said to her friend Linda, as the car headlights showed the outline of a dark mass on the roadside.

"It could be a big dog, or maybe someone hit a deer," replied Linda, also curious.

"I'm going to see what it is."

"I'm not sure I *want* to see what it is," said Linda, fearfully.

Briana and Jennifer got out of the car and walked over to what turned out to be a body.

Thomas, in full makeup, lay sprawled on his back with the glow from the car headlights defining his form.

"Oh God, it's a dead body!" exclaimed Linda.

Lisa bent to the ground, leaning over the unmoving body.

"He's so *young*," she said, brushing the hair away from his forehead.

"He's so *dead*! C'mon, let's get out of here," said Linda, in a demanding tone.

"This piece of wood is stuck in his chest. How did that happen? Get the flashlight out of the glovebox."

Reluctantly, Linda retrieved the flashlight and shown the light onto the face of the injured vampire. On cue, there was a moan, and the dark eyes opened!

"He's alive!" exclaimed Linda. "We need to get help. We need to call somebody."

"No…," came the weak voice of Penn. "Pull it out."

"What?" Lisa asked, trying to understand.

"Pull it out! Pull out the wood," the vampire pleaded, in a slightly stronger voice.

"I can't. You'll die if I pull it out. You need to go to the hospital," said Lisa.

"Pull it out!" he said, forcefully. "Pull it out!"

The dark figure grabbed at the wooden stake with one hand, trying to pull it free himself.

Hesitating, Lisa took hold of the wooden prop with both hands and yanked it from the vampire who groaned with pain and relief. Lisa stared at the sharp end of the stake that contained no blood. Linda fell to her knees beside Lisa, shaking with fear.

"Help me get him in the car!" yelled Lisa, "We need to get him to the hospital."

"Are you crazy! We need to call someone - the police or 9-1-1," Linda argued.

"No, help me," Penn pleaded. "I can't go to a hospital."

"But you're hurt," said the fair Lisa, with emotion.

"No… no hospital… please," the handsome face said to Lisa.

"Linda, help me get him in the car. I'll take him home."

"You're *so* nuts! You can't take him home! What if he

dies? This isn't a stray cat or dog, Lisa!"

"I can take him to the barn using the alleyway. I can hide him in the old tac room. No one ever goes in there. C'mon, Linda, I can't lift him by myself."

"Lisa, this is so crazy. What are you going to do with him?"

"I don't know. Help me, Linda. He's too heavy." The two girls drag the wounded Penn toward the car.

"Cut, cut!" cried Singh, clapping his hands. "Good one! That's it for tonight, folks. Wrap it up."

* * *

DeRossi stood quietly on the outskirts of the activity, watching the organized chaos that ensued after Singh called a wrap for the night. People appeared from unseen places to help break down and cart off equipment to the production trailers. Thomas, Briana and Jennifer remained standing in the first light of dawn, forming a small triangle. DeRossi strained to hear what was being said between the three actors.

"Just stay away from me, you freak!" Jennifer said to Thomas, stalking away toward the parking lot.

Briana looked after her with a surprised look on her face. Thomas had no response, his mouth in a grim line.

"Do you think she remembers anything?" asked Briana, clutching Thomas' upper arm.

"Who knows what she remembers," Thomas replied.

Then, "Go get some sleep. I have to run down to Camarillo to see my mom. I'll be back later."

DeRossi watched as Thomas kissed Briana on the cheek

and took off toward the parking lot. DeRossi also wondered exactly *what* Jennifer remembered.

He stayed true to his vow to Pauline to investigate the past of the young actor, finding little of value so far. Thomas grew up the only child of a single mother, who worked several jobs and moved frequently around the Ventura area. He was popular in high school, and enthusiastic about being on the football team. After high school, he attended some classes at a local junior college, and of late, worked at the restaurant in Malibu. He was never in any trouble with the law, other than a couple parking tickets. DeRossi didn't find any red flags.

This led DeRossi to focus on Thomas himself and his behavior. It was *there* he would find the clues. He decided that this would be a good day to follow the young man to see what he was up to, while the rest of the actors and crew sought their beds.

An hour later, driving south along the Pacific on the clear, weekday morning, DeRossi kept a good distance behind the flashy Mustang. It was just after six-thirty, and the traffic bottlenecked going through Santa Barbara as drivers sped toward their destinations. Once the road led into Ventura County, DeRossi made an effort to close the gap between his car and Thomas'. He feared losing sight of him if Thomas exited the freeway. DeRossi knew that they were nearing Thomas' home turf, but the black car continued speeding south.

Suddenly, just as DeRossi feared, the Mustang crossed three lanes of traffic and exited the freeway, turning left at the top of the off-ramp. DeRossi followed several cars behind, along a tree-lined median in an upper-class neighborhood. Again, Thomas crossed lanes, turning right onto a side street. The street was a dead end, leading into the parking lot of a major hospital complex. It was a little after seven, as he watched Thomas use a badge to enter the parking structure marked 'Staff Only'.

DeRossi turned into the visitor parking lot, parking where he had a clear view of the parking structure entrance and the nearby hospital entrance. He waited and watched. Thomas emerged from the structure wearing a white lab coat over his black wardrobe pants, carrying a clipboard. He crossed the breezeway and entered the hospital through the wide, automatic doors. DeRossi debated following but decided to stay put rather than risk losing his target. He knew that Thomas would need to return to his car.

DeRossi looked at his watch again eight minutes later. He saw Thomas exit the facility, carrying the clipboard and a small plastic bag, hurrying toward the car park.

What the hell? He thought.

Once again trailing the car, DeRossi followed Thomas into the parking lot of a nearby grocery store. Thomas entered the store, returning to his car a few minutes later carrying two, potted orchids and a grocery bag.

By eight o'clock, DeRossi pursued the car into a Camarillo neighborhood, where Thomas eventually pulled into the carport in front of a small duplex. DeRossi parked down the street, watching in his car mirror as Thomas proceeded through the front door of the house. He carried one of the orchids and the bags holding the mornings' bounty.

Time passed. DeRossi decided to use the opportunity to write down everything about Thomas he had learned, including a timeline. He added all of his detailed observations from his time on the movie location, and also wrote down the comments about Thomas from people working with him on the movie. A character profile was emerging.

Lastly, he added his own thoughts about the youth, freely tapping his astute intuition. Although not defined, a picture was starting to develop. Thomas had issues.

After a couple hours, DeRossi was surprised to see Thomas come out of the house with a large, brown dog on a leash. DeRossi slouched down in the driver's seat as Thomas walked away on the other side of the street. He decided to move the car further down the block, just before Thomas returned from his walk.

The morning lapsed into afternoon. The sleuth dozed with one eye open, watching for Thomas. The time reminded him of his days as a private detective when he and his trusty camera hung out for hours in the car, waiting…just waiting.

Around two o'clock, Thomas emerged from the house wearing a change of clothes and carrying a bag. Rather than heading north toward Santa Maria, Thomas went west on a surface street that led to the Pacific Coast Highway, where the car turned south.

DeRossi kept his distance, anticipating where the young man was going. His thoughts were confirmed when Thomas turned into the parking lot of Bluestones. He watched as the young man carried the other orchid into the restaurant.

It was an hour before Thomas got back into the Mustang and headed north. He might get a couple hours of rest before hitting the movie set, in preparation for the night's filming.

* * *

The cast and crew were on the last week of night filming. They were limping toward the finish line. The excitement of being on location was long gone. Everyone wanted to go home and get back to their lives.

Dogman was on the set early. As stunt director, he felt a responsibility to make sure that the set was ready for the night's filming. He met with the props manager, going through all of the props and weapons that were called for in the script. The stake that would be used by Kurt on Thomas was designed to retract as it touched Thomas' chest. Dogman tried it several times to make sure that it was working properly.

Then, he met with the pyrotechnic manager and crew to check out the car that was rigged to catch on fire and then explode. Gas lines were wired in and would be lit at the exact moment needed, and then enough of a blast would be used to produce the illusion of an explosion. The real look of the explosion would be completed in post-production with a computer generated, special effect. Dogman inspected the rig, walking around the car.

The stunt director looked away from the car to see his three vampires in costume and makeup walking toward the set. He was glad that they would have plenty of time for a rehearsal prior to Singh getting there.

He casually ran his hand along the side of the car, barely glancing in the side window, when a small flash of red struck his peripheral vision. Curious, he opened the back door of the car and saw two, red, gasoline containers sitting on the floor of the back seat.

"Holy hell! Who put these here?! Get them out of there! This car is a freaking bomb!" Dogman yelled, with disbelief.

Turning to the pyrotechnic manager, he demanded, "Go get Singh, *now*!"

* * *

DeRossi was late to the party as he approached the volatile group of men shouting at one another. Singh, Cooper - the assistant director that replaced Alicia, and Booker stood in the circle. The pyrotechnic manager and crew all responded with denials as to how the gasoline containers got into the stunt car. DeRossi quickly got the gist of what was happening. A potentially deadly accident was foiled, but only by chance.

Standing out of the way, the three actors playing vampires realized the danger if the car had been allowed to ignite as was planned. Possibly all of them, and anyone else in close proximity to the car, would have been killed. They were all quiet with their own sobering thoughts.

Singh was determined to complete the filming scheduled for the night. He announced filming would begin at nine sharp, glaring at everyone with dissatisfaction as he temporarily left the set.

Indeed, all hands were on deck and filming was ready to begin at nine. The mood of the night was tense, waiting for the other shoe to drop.

Surprisingly, the filming progressed, completing the choreographed fight segments in record time. Right before midnight, the gas lines on the car were ignited and the small blast was set off, producing a loud bang and a bright light.

DeRossi stayed out of the way but was never far from Thomas. Singh called for an hour lunch break, with filming to resume at one thirty. DeRossi followed at a distance as Thomas walked back to his trailer. He smiled when he saw that Briana was there waiting for her co-star.

* * *

"Hi," said Thomas, putting his arms around Briana, and giving her a kiss.

He pulled her into the trailer and closed the door. "What are you doing here? I thought you had the night off and would be catching up on your sleep."

"Some of the crew were talking in the lounge. I heard about the stunt car and Singh going ballistic."

"Yeah, that was freaky. It was Dogman who found the gasoline. They never found out who did it."

"Thomas, I'm scared. These things always happen when you're on set."

"Come here. Don't be scared. Dogman is double-checking everything," he said, pulling her into an embrace. "Not to mention DeRossi. I can't turn around without bumping into him. He's been on set all night… him and his camera."

"Thomas, are you sure you're, all right?"

"I'm okay, don't worry. Go back to the hotel and get some sleep," he said, pulling her toward the door. "C'mon, I'll walk you out to your car."

When Thomas got back from seeing Briana off, he sprawled out across the bed at the back of the trailer. He had a half hour before he needed to be back on set.

He had zoned out but came alert when he thought he heard something outside. Suddenly, there was a flash at the front of the trailer, followed by a whomping sound as light came in the front windows. Thomas was off the bed and running toward the front of the small space.

He discovered the light coming in the windows was from flames of fire surrounding the coach. Smoke started coming in through every crack from floor to ceiling. Thomas went for the door, only to realize that the handle was jammed. He balled his fist and punched the window in the door. The hard plastic cracked but didn't break. Thomas could feel the heat and see the flames enveloping the outside of the door. He ran to the back of the trailer seeking a window that he could open or push out. There was a small, rectangular window over the bed.

Jumping on the bed, Thomas pushed the window panel to the side, only to have clouds of black smoke pour in. Blinded by the smoke, he pushed out the small screen on the window and realized his body would not be able to squeeze through the opening.

Desperate in the heat and smoke, he ran back to the door, using all the strength in his legs to push against the door in an attempt to pry it open. Heat was coming from every surface he touched. He yelled out for help, knowing that everyone was back at the set. How quickly the flames were beginning to penetrate the walls of the trailer!

It's strange the things that come to one's mind when it's the end. Thomas thought of his mother. This would be hard for her. He thought of Briana and her unselfish love for him. He let his mind drift to Malibu beach on a cool night, when the moon was shining on the waves and, as he ran, the sea breeze blew against his face…

* * *

DeRossi saw Thomas take Briana to her car and return to the trailer. Reviewing the events of the long day, he slowly walked back toward the set. The next scene to be filmed was Penn getting run through with a stake. He was going to check with Booker to make sure there was no possibility of another accident.

Abruptly, he heard an indescribable sound, causing him to turn around and look back toward the parking lot. An orange glow was emanating in the darkness from the far side of the lot. DeRossi knew at once what was happening, as he sped back toward Thomas' trailer.

As he approached the inferno, he realized the trailer was engulfed with Thomas inside. He couldn't get to the door, which was fully inflamed. He ran to the back of the trailer and climbed the scalding metal ladder to the roof. He grabbed the air conditioning unit and pulled it away from its fasteners, throwing it to the ground. He tore away the flashing and lowered himself into the burning trailer.

Once standing inside, he couldn't see for the choking, black smoke. He heard a groan and moved toward where he thought the door was, tripping over Thomas.

Grabbing the slim man under his arms, he worked to get him off the floor.

"Thomas, get up!" he yelled, continuing to pull at the body. "Get up!"

DeRossi felt Thomas trying to stand and was able to prop him up, moving him toward the opening in the roof of the trailer. He slapped Thomas in the face, trying to get him to a more responsive state.

"Thomas, I'm going to boost you up. You need to pull yourself through the hole in the roof, do you hear me?!" he yelled, over the noise of the burning fire.

DeRossi grabbed Thomas around the knees and lifted

him toward the opening. He could feel Thomas struggling to pull himself through the small, square space. Seconds flew by as Thomas worked himself up and out.

DeRossi jumped up and grabbed the frame of the opening. Thomas' hand came down toward him.

He clasped the arm and Thomas pulled him out.

The roof of the trailer was collapsing under the weight of the two men. Thomas took the lead and jumped to the ground using the landing technique Dogman taught him. DeRossi followed.

Both coughing the smoke out of their lungs, they went to the grassy parkway and collapsed onto the ground. They saw that the trailer was fully engulfed in flames. Thomas heard an approaching siren. People were arriving, running from the nearby movie set.

Thomas looked closely at DeRossi, thinking that no human could have done what he had just done and live through it. Realizing that DeRossi was immortal like him, Thomas wondered how he hadn't seen it sooner. It was time to take a chance. His secret was too much to bear alone, and this person had saved him.

"Someone knows what I am, and they're after me. I don't know why," Thomas revealed.

"Yes, that's pretty obvious. Sometimes it's hard to know why. Sometimes it's just territorial," he explained. "Don't worry, we'll find out who it is."

Then, "My friends call me Carlin."

"Thank you, Carlin, for hanging around."

12

Wrap Party

When Briana returned to her hotel room after her midnight visit to Thomas, she remained in her yoga pants and t-shirt as she fell onto the bed. She was physically and emotionally exhausted from the ongoing change between daytime to nighttime sleep cycles. Almost immediately she fell into a deep, dreamless sleep.

She awoke suddenly to a pounding on the door to her room. Glancing at the clock on the bedside table, it reported two-fifteen. She sat up, startled awake in the dark room. She reached for the lamp and turned on the light. She immediately thought of Thomas and the possibility of another accident on the filming set; or maybe it *was* *Thomas* at the door.

The pounding continued as Briana crawled from the bed and went to the door.

"Who is it?" she asked.

"It's Alicia. I came to get you. We need you on the set."

Briana hesitated before removing the chain on the door. The voice *did* sound like Alicia, but she hadn't been seen with the crew since the night filming began.

In fact, she hadn't been around since the accident with Thomas running through the trees. There were rumors about her being fired, but they weren't confirmed by anyone of authority.

"Briana, open up. Singh wants you to do a retake with Thomas before dawn. You need to get to wardrobe and makeup."

Convinced, Briana opened the door and a person resembling Alicia pushed her way into the room. Briana gasped at the sight of the assistant director and retreated into the room's interior.

This wasn't the Alicia that Briana remembered. The woman's clothing was all black – clingy, black pants and a loose, black sweatshirt with a hood. Her previously bright, cropped hair was dyed black. She wore dark camouflage makeup on her face and black eyeliner, which emphasized her crazed, black eyes. Athletic gloves allowed her fingers free movement, and in her right-hand Briana saw a glint of silver – a hunting knife with a long, serrated blade.

Nothing needed to be said. The hairs stood up on the back of her neck and Briana knew at once that she was in mortal danger.

Briana moved backwards to stand against the coffee bar where her phone was charging. She knocked the small coffee pot onto the floor, distracting Alicia for the seconds she needed to slip the phone down her shirt into her bra next to a pounding heart.

"Please, let me go. Just leave. I promise I won't say anything to anyone."

"That's not possible, Briana," Alicia said, as she moved closer with the knife. "I need you to be the star of my last film. A death scene on a bridge at sunrise. It's the dream role for any actress. We're going for a little ride. Get your shoes on. You're driving."

"I'm not going anywhere with you!" Briana mustered, defiantly.

"I can kill you here, Briana. Don't push me!"

Leaving no doubt in her sincerity, she moved the knife deftly from one hand to the other. "Now grab your car keys and get out the door. We're going down the back stairs to the parking lot."

* * *

Thomas and DeRossi sat on the grassy parkway watching the firemen put out the fire that was burning the skeletal remnants of Thomas' trailer. The fire crew made quick work of it with water streaming from their thick hoses. Plumes of smoke, which changed from black to white, rose into the air as the spray hit the searing wreckage.

The entire film crew had migrated from the nearby movie set to the now crowded parking lot. No one was talking other than a few exchanged whispers. Everyone knew that it was the trailer assigned to Thomas that had gone up in flames.

Dogman came to join the smoke singed DeRossi, offering him a hand up, then assisting Thomas.

"What happened?" Dogman asked, afraid that he already knew, taking in the smoke-stained clothing on both men.

"Thomas was in the trailer, and someone lit a fire. We were just lucky to get him out in time," DeRossi said, downplaying the close call they both had escaping the inferno.

The fire captain approached the three men. "Who's in charge here?" he demanded.

Dogman looked around to find Singh rapidly approaching, seeing the top of his red turban bobbing through the crowd. He pointed to Singh.

"Are you the person in charge?" the fireman asked Singh.

"Yes," Singh replied. "I'm the director for this movie crew."

"Do all of these trailers belong to you? Do you have

permits to park them in this parking lot?"

"They're owned and rented by the studio for the filming. Our location manager made the arrangements to use the back of the parking lot for the trailers. We have a contract."

"Well, this fire was set deliberately. We found an empty gasoline can. We'll get our investigators out here in the morning, but there's no doubt in my mind that this was arson. We're going to have to get the police involved and get a police report filed."

"I'll put a call in to the studio first thing in the morning. We have insurance for these things. We'll need to get the location manager and studio legal department involved."

"Was anyone inside the trailer when the fire started?" asked the fireman.

"I don't know," replied Singh. "I just got here."

"Thomas was," volunteered a cameraman standing nearby, as he pointed to Thomas, DeRossi and Dogman.

The fireman walked over to Thomas.

"This was your trailer?"

Thomas nodded.

"You were inside when the fire started? How did you get out?"

"The door was jammed. DeRossi, here, helped me get out through the air conditioning vent on the roof."

"You were lucky. These things go up pretty fast. They're basically made of plywood and plastic. Don't take off, you'll need to give a statement as to what happened. If someone knew that you were inside and set the fire, that would make it attempted murder."

"You'll have our full cooperation," Singh chimed in.

However, the look that he threw Thomas and DeRossi said something else. He thought from the beginning that casting Thomas for the movie was a mistake. He believed that the young man brought a disruptive, black curse to *his* production. DeRossi was another problem, a spy for Pauline usurping his control.

He would be glad when this shoot was over. Never had so many catastrophes happened on a movie production.

Thomas pulled his phone from his pocket when it buzzed, indicating a new message. He glanced at it and saw that there was a text from Briana. He opened the screen to see the word '*bridge*'.

Thomas pulled DeRossi aside, showing him the lighted screen. At first DeRossi seemed confused looking at the one-word message. His confusion was replaced by a sense of alarm. He started taking steps backwards, trying to fade into the crowd.

Thomas followed him.

Once on the outskirts of the parking lot, DeRossi turned to Thomas with some urgency, "I think she is asking for help, but didn't have time to send the whole message."

Thomas stared at his newfound friend with renewed fear.

"Whoever started this fire tonight probably thinks that you went up in flames, and now they've gone after Briana. Where was she going when she left you?" DeRossi asked.

"She was going back to the hotel. She said that she was tired."

"C'mon, we'll take my car!"

When they arrived at the hotel parking lot, Thomas was the first to notice that Briana's red Lexus was gone. DeRossi parked and they raced to the doorway leading to the stairs, which was the nearest access route.

Once on the second floor, they found Briana's door locked. Thomas pounded on the door while calling out Briana's name. After no answer, DeRossi sped downstairs to the hotel desk to get help. The manager hurried upstairs with DeRossi. Opening the door, they found the hotel room empty.

* * *

Alicia instructed Briana to drive down Main Street and get onto the freeway ramp leading south toward Santa Barbara. There were few other cars on the road at this early, morning hour. Alicia demanded a higher speed as the car's headlights pierced the darkness.

"Where are you taking me?" Briana asked, in a stressed voice.

"It's not very far. We're heading to the coast. I want a scenic, ocean view for my last film."

"I still don't understand all of this. Why are you doing this to me?"

Briana thought that if she could keep the woman talking, she might be able to talk Alicia into letting her go. Previously, they had a good relationship while working on the movie; yet, this didn't seem to be the same person.

"Why? Because it's time for me to end this existence, time to build a new identity, and start a new life far away from here. I've done it many times over the years. Our kind can't stay in one place very long - a few years here, a few years there. This life was interesting, where I could use some of my physical abilities in the stunt work. It's over now. The next stop is a tent in Egypt where I'll meet a friend from a century ago. I just have a few loose ends to tie up and you're a part of that."

"What do you mean by 'our kind'?"

"We are the undead. The ancient others that live among you. We are the vampires."

Briana had no comeback for *that*. This was not the fantasy of a movie set with fake blood and fangs. Alicia was real, sitting next to her, holding a knife. Briana glanced into the face of her abductor, and saw the determined, soulless eyes for the first time.

"Yes, the heat that comes from your body is a calling card for us...fresh, young blood that is hard to resist. For now, it's a distraction. I will finish my film and post it on the Internet for the world to see. It will show the end of Briana Stillwood, just as there was the end of Thomas Johnson. After that, I will just disappear."

The car swerved to another lane, which led to the embankment, but Briana quickly reacted to steer back into the lane. She took in Alicia's meaning, hoping against hope that her conclusion was wrong.

"Thomas?" Briana said, in a whisper.

She thought of the text message that she managed to send while retrieving her shoes in the closet, before leaving the hotel with Alicia. She knew now that hope was lost for anyone coming to help her.

"Thomas is gone - burnt to a crisp. I snuffed him out before he had time to come into his own as a vampire. We don't need any younger ones."

She paused, in remembrance, "I recognized what he was at the casting meeting with Singh. Thomas was slow to react when his sleeve caught on fire. He had no injury when the heavy light bar came down on him, and then his quick recovery after falling fifty feet onto a marble floor. He also had an immediate reaction to the silver chain in the makeup trailer. It was all too obvious.

"I tried to scare him off with a glass of blood that I left in his trailer, but he didn't take the hint.

No, he persisted.

Nothing else worked, so I had to burn him - toast him to ashes. You're just a silly, little fool denying what all of your senses should have told you. You are in love with a vampire."

Briana drove on into the darkness, keeping her eyes on the road. She was stunned. Her mind was melting. Could all of this possibly be true?

Yes, in her heart she knew that it was true.

She thought of the handsome Thomas with the cool, pale skin and the mesmerizing eyes; a picture of him wet, cold and deathly pale, driving home in the car from the incident at the Santa Monica Pier; and his quickness and strength in saving the father and girl from drowning.

She'd seen him carry Jennifer with one arm and little effort. There was a smell of alcohol on his breath that night when they drove Jennifer to the hospital in her unconscious state. Had he taken Jennifer's blood? Jennifer told her that she had anemia. Most of all, Jennifer avoided Thomas like a disease when she returned to the movie set, calling him a freak.

Then there was the fact that Briana never saw Thomas

eat or drink anything.

"You know it's true, don't you, Briana?" Alicia demanded.

Briana's thoughts moved in flashes over the past two months. Her Aunt Joey had never warmed to Thomas. She had been worried and reserved at Briana's reaction to him, but Briana dismissed it. She knew of Thomas' frequent trips away from the hotel at night. Where had he been going – to get blood? Thomas usually stayed to himself on the set, never mingling with the crew. She was always worried about his secrecy – the places he would never let her go, the wall between them.

A heartbeat…she had never heard a heartbeat when laying her head against his chest.

Oh no, she thought, oh no, as she drove on toward the dawn.

* * *

Thomas and DeRossi looked around the empty hotel room. Other than the unmade bed and the coffee maker on the floor in front of the counter, there were no other clues to the girl's disappearance. Thomas spotted Briana's small, sequined purse on the bedside table.

"Look at this. She wouldn't drive anywhere without her purse."

"Thomas, can you think of anyone that would want to kill you or Briana?

"I know that someone on the set knows what I am. I knew *that* when a glass of blood was left in my trailer. There was something metallic in the blood. It burned my skin off when it splashed on me. That was right after we got up here on location."

"Pauline told me that you had a death threat with a note. That's why she hired me to try to find out what was going on with all the accidents."

"I couldn't tell anyone about the blood. I couldn't tell anyone that someone knew I wasn't human. I told them it was a death threat. I couldn't figure out who was after me, but I felt that I was being hunted. For a while, I thought it was you."

DeRossi smiled, "It *did* take me a while to put it all together."

Colin was walking by the open hotel room door on his way back from the set, when he saw Thomas.

"Hey, what's going on, man? Geez, what a weird night! You could've been killed with that fire," he said, sauntering into the room.

He was a little surprised to see DeRossi there. "Where's Briana?"

"We don't know. We're looking for her. Have you seen her?" DeRossi asked.

"I saw her around dinner time, but not since then. Is she missing? Man, I think Singh is right - this film is cursed. This has been one gothed-out night with Dogman talking about the car being rigged to explode, the trailer fire and Kurt saying that he ran into Alicia at the barn."

"What!" Thomas and DeRossi said, in unison.

"What about Alicia?" asked DeRossi.

"Yeah, man. Kurt said that he ran into Alicia outside the barn. He said he didn't recognize her at first. Her hair was dyed black, and she was wearing dark, grease paint on her face. She just ran off when he called her. Weird, man!"

"Let's go!" DeRossi called to Thomas, already on his way out the door.

"Hey, where're you goin'?" Colin asked in surprise, as Thomas raced after DeRossi.

DeRossi already had the car started as Thomas jumped into the front seat. Next, he pulled out of the parking lot going toward the freeway.

"Where are we going?" asked Thomas.

"Get your phone out and do a search. Look for bridges. We're in Santa Barbara County," De Rossi commanded. "Look for bridges in Santa Barbara County."

Thomas worked his phone as DeRossi drove through the darkness. The full moon hung low in the sky, sometimes obstructed by slow-moving clumps of gray clouds.

"I've heard talk here and there about Alicia over the years. She arrived in Hollywood about fifteen years ago, quickly getting a reputation as a stunt actor. No jump was too high, no climb was too steep, and no fall was too dangerous for her. She's known for pushing the envelope.

"Then she bought that ranch up in Topanga Canyon and built the stunt training facility. The land alone is worth millions. No one knows where she got the money. Most of these young actors coming to Hollywood don't have five grand to pay for stunt training; yet, the business survived and put out some good stunt actor.

"Did you find a list of bridges yet?"

"Not so far. These sites are full of advertising; and the bridges they're listing aren't anywhere near here," Thomas answered.

"Keep looking. Try another site," DeRossi ordered.

"There was other quiet talk about Alicia," DeRossi continued. "Most people assumed that she was gay with her strong, hard attitude. I never thought she was gay. She was known to be dedicated to her craft professionally but hung around with some unsavory characters in her private life; and there was no evidence of the gay lifestyle. She was totally apolitical and didn't mingle with the gay crowd.

"What she *really* wanted was to direct her own films. When Checkmate Studios offered her a job as stunt director she jumped at the chance. Then she moved up to assistant director in action movies, many times directing the action scenes. That's why her and Singh work well together. She loves the action scenes, and he doesn't mind delegating some of the work. She was on her way up in the eyes of the studio.

"Crazy that she would give it all up while working on this vampire movie. Thomas, the *only way* she would know that you're a vampire is if she's one herself."

"You think Alicia is a vampire?" asked Thomas, surprised.

"Well, that would answer a lot of questions, wouldn't it?" DeRossi posed, looking over at Thomas. "We are a small, guarded community mingling among the living in this world. Some of us know each other and have formed ties, but it could mean a fight to the end to expose another vampire. The good and bad of us exist through a sacred secrecy. An exposer will be hunted. It's the code."

* * *

As the highway led down from the hills and curved its way to the Pacific coast, the first hues of dawn appeared at the horizon. Briana drove on, trying not to think of what lay ahead. Alicia was restless in the seat next to her, still clutching the knife and frequently looking at the large duffle bag in the back seat. It was previously stashed in the shrubbery at the end of the hotel parking lot. She had retrieved it prior to getting into the car.

Briana was afraid to guess at what was in the bag.

"It's not much further, now. I think you'll appreciate the breathtaking location that I've chosen for our film. The bridge was built in the 1930's on the old 101 Highway. It's not used for traffic, anymore. The view of the ocean is spectacular and is frequently used by photographers."

"I will be in your film. Just let me go afterwards. I promise not to report you," Briana pleaded, trying to bargain with the wayward director.

"Let you go? I can't let you go. The climax of the film is Briana Stillwood falling from the bridge to her death – it's over eighty feet to the rocks below."

Briana didn't respond, but her mind was racing. She knew that Alicia would have to let her out of the car, which might be her only chance to escape. She planned to try to get away - away from this nightmare.

The car passed the signs for Gaviota State Park. They were north of Santa Barbara going south. The darkness made it hard to see any features along the roadside. The area was rural and devoid of any houses, or stores and the other side of the highway was all farmlands.

"Here it is. Pull over!" Alicia commanded, suddenly.

Briana sharply slowed her speed and went off the road onto a wide, gravel parkway, bringing the car to a stop.

Alicia leaned over to the back seat, unzipping the duffle

bag. After a moment, she produced what looked like a soft, red cloth.

"Here, take off those awful clothes and put this on. This should flow out nicely from your body as you fall. Hurry up, take your clothes off!"

Briana pulled off her t-shirt, exposing the cell phone tucked into her bra. Alicia instantly grabbed it.

"Smart move, honey; but you won't be needing this."

She let down the car window and threw the phone as far as she could into the tall, dry, roadside brush.

Briana put the sleeveless red dress over her head and pulled it down to her waist. Then she wiggled out of the black yoga pants, pulling them off over her shoes. Alicia leaned toward her, caressing the deep V-neckline, running her gloved hand toward Briana's breasts.

"Red is your color, Briana," she said, softly.

In one motion, Briana opened the car door and jumped out. She took off down the gravel parkway. Seeing Alicia opening her door as she looked back over her shoulder, she ran headfirst into the tall brush along the road, desperately looking for a place to hide. She continued to run as fast as she could over the uneven ground, while staying clear of the cliff that led to the beach below.

Briana would never understand how outmatched she was. The vampire chasing her had precise vision in the dim light, acute hearing for any footstep in the brush, and the speed and endurance that a human girl could never match.

Alicia was upon her in seconds, bringing her down with the force of a lioness on its prey. The air was knocked out of Briana's lungs as she crashed to the ground with great force. Her cause was lost as her world went black.

* * *

As DeRossi's car sped along in the night, Thomas finally found a list of California bridges on his phone.

"This is a really long list," he said, as he scrolled down searching for bridges in Santa Barbara County. "Here's one on Route 154."

"Great, we already passed the turn off for the San Marcos Pass. That goes up through the hills and comes out in Santa Barbara."

"Should we go back?" asked Thomas.

"Do you see any others?

Thomas continued to go through the list.

"Here's one in Goleta. It's the Arroyo Hondo Old 101 Bridge. It says it's on the Old Coast Highway over Arroyo Hondo Creek. It's closed to traffic since the new road was built, but it's open to pedestrians. Here, look at the picture. It's an arched bridge that looks pretty long and it's right by the ocean. It says it's been used for TV commercials."

DeRossi took his eyes off the road long enough to look at the picture.

"I think that might be it. What if Alicia told Briana that she was going to take pictures on a bridge?" The photographer in him came out, "This would be a great backdrop. It looks classical and very dramatic."

They drove on. DeRossi thought they couldn't be that far behind Alicia and Briana, *if* they had stayed on the highway.

"Keep an eye out on the side of the road for Briana's car."

The road leading toward the coast had many twists and turns as it passed through the hills, so DeRossi couldn't drive at the speed he wished. Once out of the hills, he increased his speed along the coast. He knew they were less than a half hour away from the old bridge.

Thomas kept his eyes on the parkway looking for the red car.

"There it is! You passed it!" Thomas exclaimed.

The road curved away from the coast as the car passed the bridge.

"You missed it!" Thomas yelled, in desperation.

They were on a major highway with a dividing median for opposing traffic. There was no place to turn around. DeRossi put his foot on the breaks hard. The car screeched, went onto the parkway and came to a halt.

"We'll have to get to the bridge from this side," said DeRossi, stating the obvious.

The two rescuers made their way from the car, and then down the slope from the highway.

As they approached the bridge, both saw the frightening sight of Briana. She was alone, toward the middle of the bridge, propped up against the railing. Her head was drooping down on her chest. Even now, in the dim light, they could see the red of the dress.

* * *

When Briana's consciousness returned, she opened her eyes to the first light of the day. The sun had not yet risen, but she realized that her nightmare continued. She looked out to the highway, only a short distance away. She saw the headlights of passing cars, with drivers ignorant of her plight and too far away to help.

Her hair had been unbraided and fell along both sides of her head to her shoulders. A trickle of blood was making its trek from her forehead to the side of her face, but she couldn't reach it. Her hands were bound behind her with some kind of rope.

So, this was the bridge, she thought. Briana was tied to the concrete railing, somewhere near the middle of the span. It was a long bridge and wide enough for two lanes of cars. It was as abandoned as she felt. Briana's back was to the ocean, but she could hear the surf echoing from below. Alicia's red dress did little to protect her from the chilly sea breeze. She shivered…or was she trembling with fear?

Briana turned her head to see Alicia further down the bridge working with a camera on a tripod, positioning both at the perfect angle for filming. Once satisfied, she reached into the duffle bag, extracting a second camera and another smaller tripod. She strode off down the bridge to the end, where she climbed onto the edge of land overlooking the deep gully under the bridge.

Alicia worked hastily, knowing that her time was limited before the sun would rise in the east. She hoped to capture the ecstasy of the golden sky, and the sun's first rays on the charcoal gray waters, as Briana plunged from the bridge.

* * *

DeRossi and Thomas decided to split up. Thomas would go for Briana, and DeRossi would go down the gully to position himself under the bridge.

DeRossi struggled down the rocky slope. His shoes were not fit for rock climbing, but he powered on through the brush. Looking up at the great concrete arches, he tried to position himself under the middle of the span. If by chance Briana or Thomas did fall, his goal was to catch them.

Thomas, on the other hand, crouched near one end of the bridge. He could see Briana and saw that her head was up, which he thought was a good sign. At least he wouldn't be trying to rescue her when she was unconscious. He saw no sign of Alicia.

It took him less than two seconds to dash to Briana's side. Immediately, he began working on the stiff plastic rope that was restraining her around the waist.

Briana was crying with joy, "She said that she burned you!"

"She tried. She set my trailer on fire and jammed the door. DeRossi pulled me out."

"DeRossi?"

Thomas glanced up to see Alicia running toward him at full speed, pulling off the sweatshirt to reveal a black sports bra. Seeing her advance, Thomas moved away from Briana, out to the center of the expanse.

As she continued to accelerate, Alicia hit Thomas with a force that propelled him backwards by fifty feet. Briana could do nothing but watch, letting out a sharp scream when Thomas was hit. At once the stunt woman was on Thomas, literally picking him up and throwing him at the railing on the far side of the bridge.

Thomas felt himself teeter on the thick, concrete rail before his body fell backwards over the side. Briana screamed again, fearing him lost to whatever lay below.

Not lost, Thomas hung by his hands from the side of a juncture of one of bridge's classic arches, taking a moment to recoup. He knew that Alicia probably thought he fell. Hand over hand, he worked his dangling body along the exterior of the bridge, trying to get closer to Briana. He could hear Briana screaming at Alicia, hysterically cursing her.

Once in a stable position, Thomas swung his legs and pulled himself up to stand on the bottom of the outside railing. In one leap, he was over the railing, attacking the unsuspecting Alicia from behind. He put a choke hold around her neck, but the woman effortlessly flipped him to the ground, pinning him beneath her. She pulled the knife from her belt, brandishing it before his face.

"I thought I was done with you!" Alicia screamed in fury.

"Let Briana go if it's me you want," Thomas demanded.

"No, I want you both. I know what you are. Did you think that you could fool an old one? How dare you come onto my set! Briana will be the revenge for those studio hacks that fired me. My film will go viral on the Internet leaving a bad taste in people's mouths. Briana will be dead, and the film will remain unfinished.

"See this knife, Thomas? It's made of the purest silver from mines in the old country. It's helped me defend myself through the decades from our kind, and all others that came against me. If fire didn't work to get rid of you, maybe this will."

Alicia raised her arm preparing to stab the knife into Thomas. Briana saw her chance. Bringing her leg up, she kicked Alicia's arm and the knife went flying.

Frustrated, Alicia turned to vent her wrath on Briana. Thomas got to his knees and grabbed Alicia by her lower legs. With an upward push, he propelled her over the concreate railing.

Thomas and Briana heard Alicia's echoing scream of fury as she descended to the floor of the gully, followed by a sickening thud from below.

Shocked by the events, Briana could only think that it could have been her on the ground below.

Tears of relief began to flow as Thomas worked to untie her.

"Thomas!" DeRossi called from below.

Thomas looked over the railing to see the prone, unmoving body of Alicia at DeRossi's feet.

"Is she finished?" Thomas called down.

"Probably not, but she will be," DeRossi yelled back.

Thomas stood with his arm around Briana, watching the sky change colors as the sun rose. They saw DeRossi build a mound of brush down by the surf. He carried Alicia's motionless form, placing it on the dried chaparral. He lit the brush on fire.

Soon, DeRossi joined Briana and Thomas on the bridge. They all were lost in their own thoughts as the form of the old vampire disintegrated in the fire below. They watched as the smoke and ashes flew away on the sea breeze.

* * *

Singh was in his element as he gave his speech at the wrap party. The filming was finished and 'in the can', as they say in Hollywood. The movie was now in post-production, where it would be refined to a final product over the next few months. The cast and crew, so bonded during the filming, would now all go their separate ways. It was time to go on to the next project.

Some would work together again, going off to film on a new location — probably minus the vampires.

Thomas stood on the sidelines as Briana took her accolades. She was a star. She had hugs and a present for all – a small ceramic tile, with "Vampire Lost" blazed across the top in a gothic font. Thomas made sure to get one for himself. There was the enhanced picture of Briana and him posing before the gnarled tree, completing the tile's artwork. He thought back to that day in the casting office, which seemed so long ago, though only a few months had passed. He had grown and changed.

Later, Thomas and Briana drove to a secluded beach in Malibu. He brought a blanket and a Thermos with hot coffee for Briana. They settled close together on the blanket spread out on the sand and looked down the embankment where the waves were hitting the shore. The full, harvest moon ascended, spilling light on the surrounding clumps of clouds and the Pacific below. The occasional sound of a seagull interrupted the rhythm of the surf coming in, encroaching on the beach.

"You brought me here to say goodbye, didn't you?" Briana asked.

She knew he had been very quiet in the car on the drive to the ocean.

Thomas did not respond.

"You can't have a girlfriend, can you?" she said, quietly.

"No," he shook his head sadly. "No, it's not in the cards."

"Can we at least be friends?" she pleaded, with some soft desperation.

"We will always be friends. I promise," replied Thomas. "For the most part though, I don't have friends, not anymore. Not in the way you would think of it. I just move from day to day. I exist."

"Can you tell me more?"

"More than you already know?" he asked, memorizing her face in the moonlight. "It's better that you don't have the gory details. It's dangerous, as you've already seen. Threats are always a possibility. I want you to be safe. You need to go on with your life, and your career. Remember me as a guy that was lucky enough to be in a movie with you. I know that I'll never forget it. I'll still be thinking of you a hundred years from now, but it's time for me to exit the stage."

Silent tears ran down Briana's face, and he gently brushed them away while holding her close.

"I want you in my life," she demanded. "I don't care about whatever makes you different."

"You *would* care if you knew the reality of this existence. You *would* care as time passed. We are from different worlds that can't go on together - not for any length of time. Time would become the enemy," he lamented.

As the night passed, they held onto each other, listening to the ocean and watching the moon on its path through the heavens.

Postproduction

No one can predict how their lives, or their existence will go. Destiny has its way of pointing one in unexpected directions. Thomas was settling in on one of these unintended paths.

He was now in partnership with Carlin DeRossi - yes, that unlikely guy that just kept showing up. Together, they opened a private detective agency, with Thomas learning the job from the seasoned sleuth. After the movie was completed, DeRossi decided to take the young vampire under his batwing. Cameras and videos were now being used for investigative surveillance.

During the post-production of the vampire movie, Thomas and Briana did not see much of each other. They were called in separately for voice-overs and whatever else was needed. Singh had overshot the film with extra scenes and takes, so editing had more material than they needed for a movie of a little over two hours. Shortly after the production had wrapped, Pauline Mellick offered Briana a second starring role with a script geared for young adults.

Checkmate Studios had also offered Thomas prospects in upcoming projects if he wished to pursue acting. Much to Maggie Finchlock's dismay, Thomas decided to walk away. As far as Hollywood was concerned, he would become the one-time male lead in an early Briana Stillwood movie.

Thomas decided to leave home, feeling that he needed to start distancing himself from his mother. He moved into the third bedroom of DeRossi's luxury condominium in North Hollywood. Getting blood for his subsistence was no longer a problem as DeRossi had well-established sources. He was still close enough that his mother was adjusting to his independence. He visited her frequently, taking the aging Pismo for walks and spending the night in his old *bedroom.*

His new lifestyle allowed for a more nocturnal existence which suited Thomas and DeRossi. They worked from afternoon until late at night, depending on what the job required. The DeRossi Investigative Agency received much of its business from online sources, and referrals from the Hollywood Police Department. Pauline Mellick had also supplied some unexpected business.

Thomas frequently returned to Bluestones in Malibu. He and DeRossi sometimes used the restaurant for meetings with clients. Many times, he brought Mrs. Rielly an orchid or roses, which always brought a smile to her face. They were friends now, both somewhat alone, and they cherished each other despite the age difference. They would chat about the restaurant business and ordinary things. He would always be her handsome, young man.

When the time came, Briana and Thomas completed the required, world-wide, publicity tour for "Vampire Lost". The tour began in Hollywood with the premier, prior to the sought-after Memorial Day weekend in America; and ending with whirlwind visits to London, Paris and Tokyo. They made the rounds of all of the national morning and late-night talk shows in New York City.

Though they had not seen each other for months, they immediately shared their prior closeness of hearts. The time together was bittersweet, and savored by both, knowing their chance for a future had passed.

Today, Thomas sat in a darkened movie theater watching Briana portray a conflicted medical student in a science fiction movie. It was his third time seeing the movie. Somehow it made him feel closer to her.

He knew that she was well on her way to transitioning to an adult film star, since she was currently on location with her third movie. As he watched a close-up scene, he remembered holding her, touching her face and kissing her. Her mannerisms and expressions were so familiar. Thomas sighed in the darkness. He wondered when he would stop missing her.

Thomas kept protective tabs on Briana and could be found frequently driving by the tall, wooden gate in front of her house. He knew what she was doing most of the time but denied that he might be stalking her. He thought of himself as a friendly shadow that could quietly intercede if danger approached. He knew she was one phone call away, but resisted even though he hadn't been able to completely let go of his love for her.

A loneliness remained in Thomas's life, even with his busy schedule. He sometimes longed for the prospect of a girlfriend, or later a family, which seemed to be forever denied. DeRossi understood all of this and tried to help by introducing Thomas to new interests, culture and supporting his enjoyment of conservation projects. DeRossi planned a trip to Europe or a 'tour of the continent', as he called it. Thomas was beginning to see that the world was his oyster. With his unnatural abilities, and the unlimited time before him, his future could follow many roadways and dreams. He knew there were others like him out there. Maybe someday he would be the one to guide a fledgling vampire. Maybe a forever companion would be found somewhere. There was always hope.

About the Author

*E*ileen Raye started on the road to being an author several decades ago, then life happened. Now a retired nurse, the blank page was calling. Ms. Raye is a supporter of the printed page, bookstores - new and used - and encourages reading for all age groups.

She currently lives in Boulder City, Nevada - near Las Vegas - with her husband. Her hobbies include reading, writing and attending a book club. Retired from a fulfilling career in nursing, Ms. Raye also enjoys gardening, jigsaw puzzles and a robust "Harry Potter" collection. Family, grandchildren and pets bring a sweetness to her life.

EILEEN RAYE

EILEEN RAYE